THROUGH
Golden Windows

By V. Gilbert Beers

Illustrated by Helen Endres

MOODY PRESS • CHICAGO

What You Will Find in This Book

© 1975 by V. Gilbert Beers
Library of Congress Cataloging in Publication Data
Beers, Victor Gilbert, 1928-
    Through golden windows.

    (The Muffin family picture Bible)
    SUMMARY: Each Bible story is followed
by a tale involving the Muffin family
which illustrates the contemporary
application of biblical principles.
    1. Bible stories, English. [1. Bible stories.
2. Christian life] I. Endres, Helen. II. Title.
BS551.2.B44   220.9'505   75-25535
ISBN 0-8024-8753-X

Printed in the United States of America
Third Printing, 1980

ISAAC—
A PROMISE BENEATH THE STARS 120

TO PARENTS AND TEACHERS

Bible storytelling at its best goes far beyond the mere telling of the Bible story. As a parent or teacher, you want your child to know what this story means, and how he can apply its truth to his daily living.

Through Golden Windows does not stop with the telling of the Bible story. It goes on, through the adventures of The Muffin Family, to help your child make the transition from Abraham to his own back yard, and beyond.

You may think at times that The Muffin Family look like rag dolls. Perhaps they are! But you and your child will recognize their adventures as your own. And you will recognize the truths that they learn from God's Word as your own, too!

Since the Bible stories are a creative retelling of the Scriptures, you may wish to use the Bible itself wherever possible as you share the adventures in this volume with your children.

BASKETS, BULRUSHES,
AND A BURNING BUSH

A Basket for the Baby

EXODUS 2:1-10

Amram was always tired when he came home. Every day he worked as a slave, making bricks for Pharaoh, king of Egypt.

One night, Amram looked especially tired and sad. "What is the matter?" Jochebed asked. "Why are you so sad?"

"Haven't you heard?" Amram asked. "Pharaoh has told his men to kill every Hebrew baby boy."

Jochebed held her little baby boy close to her. "No!" she cried. "They can't do that!"

"I'm afraid they can," said Amram. "We must do all we can to hide our baby."

Each night, Jochebed thought of some new way to hide her baby boy. Each day the king's men looked for Hebrew babies so they could kill them.

Jochebed was always so afraid. If her baby cried while the king's men were here, they would find him and kill him.

Three months went by. It was becoming harder and harder to find a new place to hide their baby.

"The king's men always look in the houses," she told Amram. "We must find a hiding place away from the houses."

6

"But where?" Amram wondered.

"I know," said little Miriam. "The king's men never go down to the river."

"Then I will make a little basket with some bulrushes," said Jochebed. "We will put our baby in the basket and hide it among the plants in the river."

It was such a good idea! Miriam helped her mother gather the bulrushes and weave them into a little basket. She watched for the king's men while her mother carried the basket down to the river and hid it among the plants.

Miriam hid nearby to watch while Jochebed went home. Suddenly, Miriam caught her breath.

"Here comes the princess!" she whispered. "She must not see our basket."

But the princess did see the basket. "Look," she said to her helpers. "There is a basket in the river. Bring it to me."

When the princess looked in the basket, she saw the baby. "What a beautiful baby!" she said. "I know what I will do! I will keep him for my own."

When Miriam heard that, she ran bravely to the princess. "I know a woman who will take care of your new baby," she said.

"Good!" said the princess. "Bring her here!"

7

Jochebed thought something terrible had happened when Miriam rushed into the house. "Mother! Mother!" she cried out. "Come with me. Hurry!"

Jochebed was even more frightened when she saw the princess holding her baby boy. What had happened? Would the princess have her baby killed?

"I want to keep this baby for my own," the princess told Jochebed. "He will be called Moses. But I need someone to take care of him. Will you do it?"

Jochebed could hardly believe her ears. God had kept her baby safe. No one would ever try to hurt him now! And she could still keep Baby Moses in her own home.

When Amram came home that night, he found Jochebed singing as she rocked their baby. "What are you doing?" he cried out. "The king's men will hear you and take our baby away!"

"Never!" Jochebed sang out. Then she told Amram all that had happened that day.

Amram shook his head as he heard these things. "Only God could do such a wonderful thing!" he said. "Perhaps God has some special work for our baby when he grows up!"

Of course, Amram could not know what important work God would have for this baby. He could not know that he would become the great Moses, who would lead all of their people from their slavery in Egypt.

WHAT DO YOU THINK?
1. How did God help Jochebed and Miriam take care of Baby Moses? Why do you think God did this?
2. How did Jochebed and Miriam help God take care of Baby Moses? Why was it important for them to do their part, too?

8

The Wishing Stump

"What are you doing, Maxi?" asked Mini Muffin. "Why do you come here every day after school to sit on this old stump?"

It was just an ordinary stump on the little hill across from the shops. Mini was sure there must be nicer places to sit, such as a chair at home.

"Why, Maxi? Hunh? Why?"

"Get lost, willya?" Maxi grumbled. "Can't you see that I'm busy?"

Mini looked puzzled. That was the unbusiest way to look busy that she had ever seen.

"Besides," said Maxi, "you shouldn't be here when I'm working at my Wishing Stump."

"Working? Wishing Stump?" asked Mini. Now she looked more puzzled.

"Stop bugging me!" said Maxi Muffin. "I'll never get that bike in the window if I don't start my wishing for today."

Mini looked across the street at the bike shop window. There was a beautiful new bike. Then she looked at Maxi. She knew that he didn't have the money to buy that bike.

"Why don't you make that your Praying Stump?" Mini asked quietly.

"Beat it, kid!" Maxi growled.

But as soon as Mini left, Maxi began to think. "Maybe she's right! I'm not getting that bike very fast on my Wishing Stump. Maybe I should make it my Praying Stump."

Maxi had just started to work on his Praying Stump when who should come along but Mr. Winkie, the owner of the bike shop. "Well, well," said Mr. Winkie. "If it isn't Maxi Muffin. But why are you sitting there on that old stump on such a beautiful day? You should be riding your bike."

Maxi looked down at the ground and gulped a big gulp. "I . . . I don't have a bike," he said. "And I don't have the money for one. That's why I'm working here on my Praying Stump."

Mr. Winkie thought for a moment or two. "Hmmmm," he said. "Seems to me you should make that your Pray and Do Stump. Why don't you finish your praying, then do something about it, like coming to the bike shop to ask me for a job. Might be a good way to get that bike!"

Maxi was so happy that he could hardly finish his work on the Pray and Do Stump. He almost got to the bike shop before Mr. Winkie.

"Did you finish your work on the Pray and Do Stump?" asked Mr. Winkie.

"Yes," said Maxi. "I asked God to help me get the bike in the window."

"Good!" said Mr. Winkie. "Now if you work hard for me after school each day, you can help God to help you get the bike."

"Oh, I will! I will!" said Maxi Muffin.

And he did!

LET'S TALK ABOUT THIS

1. Why didn't Maxi get his bike by wishing on the Wishing Stump?

2. What did Maxi do that was better than wishing for a bike? What did Mr. Winkie tell Maxi to do? Was this an answer to Maxi's prayer?

3. Why can't we simply ask God to do our work for us?

11

The Bush
That Kept Burning

EXODUS 3:1—4:17

"Why can't someone lead my people out of Egypt?" Moses wondered. Every day, as he took care of sheep, Moses thought of his people, making bricks for the king.

"They're nothing but slaves!" Moses often said. "They always will be, too, unless someone will be brave enough to lead them away from the king."

Moses' people had been slaves for many years. His father, Amram, was a slave. Moses would have been a slave for the king, too, if the princess had not found him in the river and raised him.

Now, Moses was a shepherd. It wasn't as good as being the son of a princess. But it was much better than being a slave!

Moses often thought of the day when he had killed an Egyptian who had been beating a Hebrew slave. That was when he had to run away from Egypt and come here to work as a shepherd in Midian.

Suddenly Moses' thoughts of Egypt came to an end as his sheep stirred and ran. Something was happening. The sheep seemed afraid.

Moses ran to see what it was. Then he saw a bush that had caught on fire. As Moses watched, the bush kept on burning, but it never burned up.

Moses walked slowly toward the bush, wondering at the strange sight of a bush that never stopped burning. Suddenly a Voice called out from the bush.

"Moses! Moses!"

"Who is it?" Moses asked, trembling and afraid.

"Don't come closer!" the Voice said. "Take off your sandals! You are standing on holy ground."

Moses pulled his sandals from his feet. Then he covered his face and bowed down before the bush. He knew now who was speaking.

"I am the God of Abraham, Isaac, and Jacob," the Voice said. Moses grew more afraid now. Why was God speaking to him?

"I know all about the slaves in Egypt," God said. "I am going to take them away from Egypt into a beautiful land with plenty of food."

Moses was so happy to hear this. At last God would lead His people from slavery. But what man would be brave enough to lead these people for God?

"You will lead your people!" God told Moses. "You will take them away from the king."

Now Moses was terrified. How could he make the king give up a million or more slaves?

"You know that I can't do that!" Moses complained. "I don't know how."

"Then I will help you," God said. "I will be with you."

"But what can I say to my people?" Moses asked. "How will they know that You are with me?"

"Tell them!" God said.

"They won't believe me," Moses answered.

"What is in your hand?" God asked.

Moses held up a big stick, called a rod, which he used to fight the wild animals.

"Throw it on the ground!" God commanded.

When Moses did that, the rod became a live snake. Moses was so afraid that he began to run away from it.

"Don't run!" God said. "Lift it up by the tail."

As soon as Moses touched the snake, it became a rod again.

"Will your people believe you now?" God asked. "But to make sure, reach your hand into your robe."

When Moses took his hand from his robe, it was white with leprosy. Everyone was afraid of leprosy, for it was such a terrible disease.

"Put your hand inside your robe again," God commanded.

When Moses did that, his hand was well again.

"You will see other wonderful things," God told Moses.

"But I can't talk very well," Moses argued.

"Who made your mouth?" God asked. "Now go and do what I tell you. I will help you."

By this time, Moses was frantic. "Lord! Please send someone else," he pleaded.

"If you must have someone to talk for you, take your brother Aaron with you," God said angrily.

That was all. Moses was stunned as the fire flickered and went out. There was no sound now except the hot desert wind blowing through the bushes and the bleating of Jethro's sheep.

Slowly Moses made his way home, his mind filled with many thoughts. Behind him marched the long line of sheep. But God's words kept ringing through his mind, "Go! Do what I tell you!"

Moses knew that he had no other choice.

WHAT DO YOU THINK?

1. Why do you think God chose Moses for this special kind of work? What kind of help did God offer? Why did Moses need this help?

2. What kind of excuses did Moses give for not doing what God said? What did God tell him about these excuses?

3. Why do you think that Moses had to do this work?

Treasure Hunt

"The treasure hunt is ready to begin!" said Pookie. Pookie's party had been a good one, but everyone thought the treasure hunt would be the best part of the party.

"Somewhere in town I have hidden a golden egg," said Pookie. "Actually, it's a leftover Easter egg painted gold. But when you bring it to me, I'll trade you this giant bag of Tango Mints for it."

Pookie held up the big bag of Tango Mints. That was everyone's favorite candy. Some said "ummm" and others said "yummmm," but everyone agreed it was a good prize.

"The first one to follow his directions right will find the egg," said Pookie. "The rest of you will find where it *was*. Last one back here gets the booby prize—the old egg itself!"

Pookie reached his hand into a giant cowboy hat on the table. He gave one piece of paper to Maxi, another to Mini, and four more to their friends.

"They're all different!" said Pookie. "But they all take you to the same place! Get going!"

All six started out in different directions, as their pieces of paper told them to do. As Maxi started out, he had a big smile on his face.

"I know how to do these things," he said to himself. "Just take a shortcut with every other thing on the list!"

Maxi went down to the corner to the big oak tree, just as his paper said he should. "Cross the bridge in the park," he read, "go left a hundred steps to the hickory tree and hold out your right arm. Take the street your hand points to and go to the end of it."

Maxi looked at the park. There was the bridge. But there were three hickory trees to the left of the bridge.

"It must be the biggest one," said Maxi. He ran to the tree and held out his right arm.

"Of course! Hickory Street!" said Maxi. "What else?" So Maxi ran to the end of Hickory Street.

"Now cross the stream and turn left on the street on the other side," Maxi read on the paper. "That's dumb, Pookie, why didn't you take us across the stream back near the park where there's a bridge?"

But Maxi crossed the stream, getting a little more muddy and a lot more grumbly as he went. He read the next two directions. "I know where that goes," he said. "I'll take a shortcut."

Farther and farther Maxi went from Pookie's house. At last he found himself at the city dump. "Why would Pookie send us out here?" he grumbled. "And where are the others?"

Just then Maxi saw a man working with a big yellow machine. He ran over to talk to the man.

"I'm looking for some treasure!" said Maxi.

"Sure, kid!" said the man. "You can have all you want." The man waved his arm toward the old cans and bottles. Then he laughed and laughed. Maxi didn't think it was at all funny.

Maxi was sure now that he had not followed the directions on the paper. Someone had surely found the golden egg by this time.

Maxi kicked a tin can and a mouse ran out of it. "Dumb mouse!" he grumbled. "I suppose you're looking for treasure, too!" Then Maxi headed back for Pookie's house.

18

Everyone was waiting when Maxi came back. They all looked tired, as if they had been waiting for a long time.

"Where have you been, Maxi?" said Pookie. "Mini was back in six minutes! She won the Tango Mints. But don't worry, you win the booby prize."

"I took a shortcut!" Maxi mumbled. "But I guess it wasn't so short after all. Where was the egg hidden?"

"In my cowboy hat here!" said Pookie. "The directions took all of you out to the park and around the block."

"But don't worry, Maxi," said Mini. "I'll share the Tango Mints with you."

"Dumb kid!" said Maxi.

"Who, me?" asked Mini.

"NO, ME!" said Maxi. Then everyone laughed. Even Maxi.

LET'S TALK ABOUT THIS

1. Why was it important for Moses to do exactly what God told him to do?

2. Why was it important for the treasure hunters to do exactly what their papers told them to do?

3. What happened to Maxi when he didn't follow directions? What happened to Mini when she did follow directions?

4. Why should we do what God tells us? Why should you do what your parents tell you?

The King
Who Said No

EXODUS 5:1—13:16

"No!" said Pharaoh, king of Egypt. "I will not let your people go out of Egypt!"

Moses and Aaron had come to talk with the king. They had told him that God wanted His people to leave Egypt.

The king was very angry. Moses' people were slaves. They made bricks for the king so that he could make buildings. He did not want to let his slaves go out of the land. Who else could do his work for him then?

So the king gave orders to his taskmasters. "Don't give these Hebrew slaves any more straw," he said. "Make them look for it. But they must make as many bricks as they did before."

Now Moses' people were angry at him and Aaron. "What are you doing to us?" they said. Some of them began to say some things about Moses that shouldn't be said about friends.

Moses talked to God about this. "See what is happening?" he said. "The king won't do what You said and now my own people are angry at me."

20

"Go back to the king," God ordered. "Do exactly as I say. You will see some wonderful things happen."

Moses went back to the king. "You must let my people go out of Egypt," he said.

"No!" said the king. "I will not let your people go out of Egypt. Why should I listen to your God?"

"Because He can do this!" said Moses. Aaron threw down his big stick before the king. It became a snake.

"My magicians can do that, too!" said the king. And they did, but Aaron's snake ate the other snakes. Even so, the king would not let Moses' people go away from Egypt.

Moses went back to see the king again. "You must let my people go out of Egypt," he said.

"No!" said the king. "Why should I?"

Moses told Aaron to hold out his stick toward the river. When he did, the river became blood. But the king's magicians also turned some water into blood. So the king would not let Moses' people go away from Egypt.

"Go back to see the king again," God said to Moses one day. "Tell him to let My people go away."

When the king said "no" again, God said that Aaron should hold out his hand. Suddenly, there were frogs everywhere. But the king's magicians caused frogs to come, too. So the king would not let Moses' people go away.

The next time Moses came to see the king, God caused lice to go all over the land. The king's magicians tried to do this, too, but they could not.

"Now we know that God does these things," the magicians told the king. But he still would not let Moses' people go away from Egypt.

Again and again Moses came back to see the king. Each time he told the king what God had said. "You must let my people go away from Egypt," he would say.

"No!" the king answered.

Each time Moses came, he showed the king some wonderful thing that God could do. One time the land was filled with flies. The next time, God made all the cows get sick. Then the people got sick with big sores.

By this time, the people of Egypt were afraid of Moses and his God. But the king kept on saying "no!"

Then God sent thunder and hail. It killed everything that was outside. After that God sent swarms of locusts to eat up everything that the hail had not destroyed.

"Let those people go away!" the king's people begged. "We will all be killed if you don't."

"No!" said the stubborn king.

Once more God spoke to Moses. "Hold out your

22

hand!" He commanded. When Moses did that, the land of Egypt became as dark as the darkest night. For three days the people could not go anywhere.

But still the king would not let Moses' people go. He wanted to keep them as his slaves.

Then Moses gave the king one last warning.

"Tonight, at midnight, God will pass through this land," he said. "Every Egyptian boy who is the oldest in the family will die, even your own son!"

The king was afraid. But he still said no.

It was too late to help the people of Egypt. But Moses told his own people how to keep their sons from dying that night. "Put some blood from a lamb on the doorposts of your houses. When God passes through the land at midnight, stay inside. Wherever He sees the blood, He will pass over that house."

That night, while God's people prayed and ate the lambs that they had killed, the Egyptians cried. Everything happened the way Moses had said it would. Even the king's oldest boy was dead.

Quickly the king sent for Moses. "Go!" he said. "Take your people and get out of Egypt." The king's people were afraid, too, and begged Moses and his people to leave.

Moses' people were ready and waiting to leave Egypt. Never again would they be slaves for a king who said no.

WHAT DO YOU THINK?
1. What did Moses want the king to do? Why did the king keep on saying no?
2. Why would the king have been happier if he had said yes to God? How did he get hurt by saying no?
3. How did the king's friends and the king's people get hurt because he kept on saying no to God?

23

Tony Maloney's Pony

"What a pony!" Maxi whistled.

"He's beautiful, Tony," said Mini. "I'm so glad you asked us to ride in your pony cart."

"Tony invited me first," said Maxi, "so I get to ride in the cart more than you do."

Before Mini could answer, Maxi Muffin was in Tony Maloney's pony cart. He took the reins in his hands.

"Giddap!" he shouted.

Tony's pony trotted along with the pony cart behind. Around and around the barnyard went the pony cart. First Maxi went this way. Then he went that way. He stayed in the pony cart for such a long time that Mini thought her turn would never come.

"Maxi!" she called. "You're not being fair. Poppi said you must give me my turns today."

But Maxi pretended that he didn't hear Mini. He kept on going round and round, here and there. Tony didn't like to see Maxi do this.

"Hey, Maxi," he shouted. "It's Mini's turn. Pull it in."

Maxi looked as if he had swallowed a lemon when he pulled the pony cart up to them. He sulked as he got out of the cart and watched Mini get in.

24

"Be careful!" said Tony.

"Yeah! Don't go too fast!" said Maxi, with a mischievous grin. When Maxi said that, he gave Tony's pony a sharp slap on the back.

Tony's pony was surprised by Maxi's sharp slap. He reared up with a loud whinny, then galloped across the barnyard as fast as he could go, with Mini and the pony cart bouncing behind him.

"Why did you do that?" shouted Tony. "Are you trying to get Mini hurt?"

Tony and Maxi ran after the pony cart as fast as they could go. But the pony ran faster.

Down the farm lane went the pony. Faster and faster he ran. Maxi was frightened now. What if Mini got hurt? He was so sorry that he had slapped Tony's pony. If only they could do something. But the pony was going too fast to catch him.

Suddenly Maxi and Tony saw a herd of cows crossing the farm lane. Tony's pony saw them, too. He reared up on his hind legs and ran to the side, right into the pond.

What a mess Maxi and Tony found when they ran up huffing and puffing to the pond. There was Tony's pony, wet and muddy. Tony's pony cart was covered with mud, too. And there was Mini, still sitting in the pony cart, splattered with mud, too frightened to cry.

When Maxi saw all this mess, he felt more sorry than ever. What had he done? Why did he ever do that to Tony and Mini?

"I . . . I didn't mean to hurt anyone," Maxi said to Mini and Tony, hanging his head. "I'm so sorry! Please forgive me!" Then Maxi helped Mini wipe the mud off her clothes.

It took awhile to clean the mud from Tony's pony and the pony cart as well. When they were finished, Tony smiled a big smile.

26

"All ready!" he said. "Who'll be first?"

"It's Mini's turn!" said Maxi.

Maxi smiled as he watched Mini riding around and around the barnyard in Tony's pony cart.

"Your turn now?" asked Tony.

"Not yet," said Maxi. "Let Mini have an extra long turn this time!"

LET'S TALK ABOUT THIS

1. How was Maxi like the king in the Bible story? How did the king hurt his friends and his people? How did Maxi hurt his friends?

2. Why would Maxi have been happier if he had done what he should? How would this have pleased God?

3. What did Maxi do that made the story turn out right? Why do you think this would please God?

4. What can you do to make things turn out right when you hurt your friends?

27

Songs By the Side of the Sea

EXODUS 13:17—15:19

Never before had the Egyptians seen so many Hebrew slaves in one place. There were more than a million of them!

But they were not slaves now. The king had ordered them out of the land. The king's people had begged them to leave. All of the Egyptians were afraid of Moses and his people because of the troubles that God had sent to Egypt.

"Go!" the king had said. "Get out of Egypt!"

Moses and his people were going. They wanted to get out of Egypt before the king changed his mind again.

"But where are we going?" some of Moses' people asked.

"To a new land that God has promised," said others. "Moses will lead us there."

"How will Moses know the way?"

"God will show him!"

God did show Moses where to go. Before long, a beautiful cloud appeared. It was like a tall pillar.

"God will lead us with that cloud," Moses told his people.

By day, it was a cloud. By night, it was a pillar of fire. The people knew then that God was with them at all times. How happy they were to know that God was leading them to a new land!

At last Moses and his people came to the Red Sea. Behind them was Egypt. Before them, on the other side of the sea, was the way to the land God had promised.

"But how will we get across?" some wondered.

"God will show us a way," said others.

Suddenly all the people began to panic.

"Chariots!" they cried. "The king's men have come to kill us!"

Clouds of dust rose up behind the chariots. There were hundreds of them! Closer and closer came the king's men.

"What will we do?" the people cried out. "We will all be killed."

"God will take care of us," Moses shouted to the people. "Don't be afraid."

Something strange began to happen. The pillar of cloud moved toward the king's men. It grew bigger and bigger as it moved. Then it went between the king's men and Moses' people.

The king's men could not see Moses and his people now, so they had to stop.

"Hold out your hand toward the sea!" God told Moses.

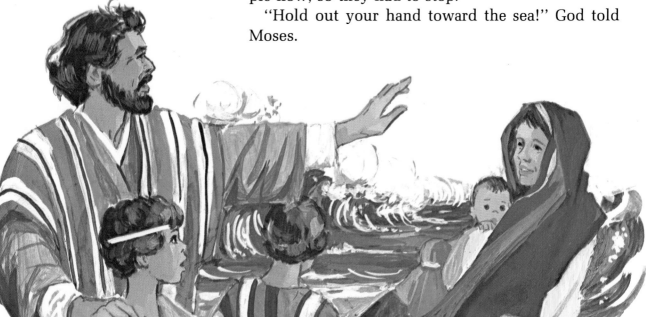

When Moses did that, a strong wind blew. The people could hardly believe their eyes. The waters of the sea began to move apart.

"Get ready to march by sunrise," Moses commanded.

All night long the wind whipped through the camp as the people made ready to march again. At last, the first rosy tints of the sunrise painted the sky and the sea. Then the people saw a great path of dry land leading to the other side.

"Through the sea!" Moses commanded.

As Moses walked through the sea to the other side, his people followed behind, looking this way and that at the water on each side of them. When the last of Moses' people had climbed safely to the other side, someone gave a shout.

"The Egyptians are coming!"

The king's men raced across the path in their chariots. But as they did, Moses stretched out his hand toward the sea, and the water rushed back into the path.

The king's men were frightened. "Go back!" they shouted. But they couldn't. The water poured over them and their chariots. There was no one to fight for the king now. Moses and his people were free.

The morning sunrise painted the mountains a rosy gold. A shaft of sunlight glistened on the sea. Then a voice began to sing. The great crowd of people joined in and the mountains and hills echoed with a song of praise to God.

The people were free! Never again would they be slaves!

And never again would they forget this great choir of voices, singing praises to God for setting them free.

WHAT DO YOU THINK?
1. What did God do for His people? Why was that such a wonderful thing for Him to do?
2. What did the people do to thank God for His goodness? How do you think God felt when He heard the great choir of voices, singing praise to Him? How do you think the king felt when he heard it?

Paddle-Boat Picnic

"What's a paddle boat?" Mini asked.

"It's fun!" said Poppi Muffin. "It's a little boat with pedals that turn some paddles. You make it go by turning the pedals round and round, like riding a bike."

"Is it like riding my bike?" asked Mini. "Can I do it, too?"

"Of course," said Poppi. "You and Maxi will be the boat's motor. This will be one of our most fun-filled picnics."

"A paddle-boat picnic," said Mommi. "Doesn't that sound like fun?"

It did! So the Muffin Family talked about their paddle-boat picnic all the way to the boathouse on the river.

Before long, the man at the boathouse had two paddle boats ready to go. He helped Mommi and Poppi into one. Then he helped Mini and Maxi into the other, along with Ruff and Tuff.

"You can go anywhere in this lagoon," said the man. "And you can go along the banks of the river. But don't go out in the middle of the river. The current is too swift."

The paddle boats were even more fun than Mini and Maxi had thought they would be. They chased Mommi and Poppi for a while. Then Mommi and Poppi chased them for a while. After that, they all went exploring along the banks of the river.

At last Mommi and Poppi pulled their boat up to a place where there was a picnic table. "We'll get lunch ready," said Mommi. "But come when we call."

Mini and Maxi waved and were off in their paddle boat. "Look!" said Mini. "There's a duck. Maybe she wants to play tag!"

Away went the paddle boat toward the duck. But the duck swam off to the side as Mini and Maxi went on by. Ruff barked at the duck. The duck gave a long quack, quack, quack at Ruff.

Maxi and Mini turned the boat around and tried again. But the duck was too fast for them. He swam off to the other side.

Again and again Mini and Maxi tried to catch up to the duck. But the duck always won. They were having so much fun that they didn't watch where they were going.

Suddenly Mini caught her breath. "Maxi!" she cried. "We're out in the river. Look! We're being carried along on the current!"

Maxi tried to turn the paddle boat around, but it was too late! The swift current of the river began to sweep them along. Faster and faster they went.

"Look out!" shouted Mini.

Maxi looked in time to see a giant log caught on some rocks ahead. But it was too late to do anything about it. The paddle boat rammed into the log, throwing Maxi and Mini into the water.

"Hold onto the log!" shouted Maxi.

"Help!" called Mini.

"Coming!" Poppi called.

Ruff and Tuff scrambled up on the big log while Mini and Maxi held onto it. In a few minutes Poppi was there with his paddle boat and had them all safely inside.

"Whew! That was close!" said Maxi later as they sat down to eat their picnic lunch.

"The Lord took care of you," said Poppi.

"So let's have a little Thank-You Time," said Mini.

Ruff and Tuff sat quietly as The Muffin Family sang a happy song about God and thanked Him for taking care of them.

"May we have another paddle-boat ride after lunch?" Maxi asked when they had finished their Thank-You Time.

"In the lagoon!" said Poppi.

"Yes," said Maxi. "In the lagoon!"

LET'S TALK ABOUT THIS

1. Why did The Muffin Family have a Thank-You Time?

2. What do you do when God has helped you? Do you have a Thank-You Time with God?

3. What do you think God wants you to do when He helps you? Why?

FOUR FRIENDS
WHO FOLLOWED JESUS

Stephen—The Man Who Looked into Heaven

ACTS 6:1—8:2

"It isn't fair," some of the Christians complained to other Christians. "Our widows aren't getting as much food as your widows."

This was true. Although the twelve apostles tried to be fair, they were just too busy. Some things didn't get done as well as they should.

Not long after Jesus had gone back into heaven, the Christians decided to share their food with their widows. The twelve apostles found it easy to do this work at first, for there weren't many Christians. Then thousands of people became Christians and soon there was too much work for the apostles to do.

"We must have a meeting and decide what to do now," said the twelve apostles.

So they had a meeting. And they invited other Christians to come, too.

"Listen," they explained to the other Christians. "We should be spending our time praying and telling others about Jesus. Why don't you choose seven other men to take care of things such as food. Be sure that they are wise and filled with the Holy Spirit."

It was such a good idea that the Christians decided to do it. They chose seven men, including Stephen.

38

Stephen was an unusually good man, filled with the Holy Spirit. Wherever Stephen went, God worked great wonders through him.

Everyone began to say good things about Stephen. That is, almost everyone. There was a group of men who hated Jesus, so they hated Stephen, too. It made them angry to see Stephen win so many people to Jesus.

"Let's get him into an argument," they said. "We are so wise that we will make him look foolish."

But when these men tried to argue with Stephen, they didn't know what to say. In his quiet, sweet way, Stephen was too wise for them. Of course, this made them even more angry.

These men paid some others to lie about Stephen. They said some terrible things about him, so Stephen was arrested and sent before the high priest and his council.

The men who lied came there, too. They had to tell the same lies to the council.

"He says things against God's house," they claimed. "He says that Jesus will tear it down and throw out Moses' laws."

"Are these things true?" the high priest asked.

When the members of the council looked at Stephen they were surprised. He didn't look the same now. His face was as bright and sweet as an angel's face.

"Let me tell you what is true," Stephen began. Then he told them again about the great men of God, such as Abraham, Jacob, Joseph, and Moses. He told them how the people of Israel had turned against God time after time, even though God had done so much for them.

"And you have done the same thing," Stephen cried out. "You have turned against God's own Son, Jesus, and have murdered Him. By doing this, you have turned against God."

The high priest and his friends were furious when they heard this. They were so angry that they began to grind their teeth.

Stephen kept on talking to them. He wasn't bothered by their anger.

"Look! I see heaven opened," he said. "I see Jesus, God's Son, standing there by God's right hand."

The men of the council were so angry they rushed toward Stephen, dragging him outside the city. They would not even bother to judge him. They would simply kill him there.

The men who lied about Stephen had to throw the stones that would kill him. But what did they care? They laid their cloaks by a young man named Saul. Then they began to throw the stones at Stephen.

"Lord Jesus," Stephen prayed, "take me to be with You."

As the stones began to strike him, Stephen prayed once more. "Lord, don't hold this wicked thing against them."

Then Stephen fell to the ground. He had gone to live forever with Jesus, the One whom he loved so much.

WHAT DO YOU THINK?
1. Why did some men lie about Stephen? Why did the men who hired them hate Stephen so much?
2. How did Stephen feel about Jesus? Why did he want to tell others about Jesus?
3. What did Stephen say about his enemies just before he died? Why did he forgive his enemies when they were hurting him?

The Tooti Frooti Shop

"He doesn't like us!" Mini Muffin whimpered. She sniffed and wiped a tear from her eye. "He said mean things to us and told us to go away."

"Yeah!" Maxi added. "He even told us not to come back there—ever again!"

Mini and Maxi had been so excited to see Mr. Middleberry put up The Tooti Frooti Shop. They had wanted to make friends with him and help him. It would be fun to be a helper in such an interesting place.

Where else could someone find a fruit stand like that? There was the old circus wagon with its striped canopy. And the baskets and jars sitting here and there looked so good filled with fruits and nuts and candies. It was certainly a fun place!

"I know that Mr. Middleberry didn't mean to hurt you," said Mommi Muffin. "Is there something you're not telling me?"

"Well . . ." said Maxi.

Maxi looked at Mini. Mini looked at Maxi.

"We didn't do it on purpose," Mini said softly.

Mommi didn't say a word. She just waited for Mini and Maxi to say what she knew they wanted to say.

"We weren't doing anything," said Mini.

"Except playing with Ruff and Tuff," added Maxi.

"But everything was all right," said Mini. "That is, until Ruff started chasing Tuff."

"And Tuff started climbing things," said Maxi.

"Like Mr. Middleberry's shop?" asked Mommi.

"But Tuff only knocked over a little basket of oranges," said Mini.

"Of course, they did fall against the pecan basket," said Maxi.

"And it fell against the candy jars and knocked them over," said Mini.

"It was really neat, Mommi," Maxi went on, "you should have seen all those candies and nuts and things rolling across the floor."

Maxi almost looked as if he thought it was fun when he said that. But he quickly looked sad again. He knew that Mommi didn't think it was much fun!

"And, what did you do then?" Mommi asked.

"Well, Ruff and Tuff ran toward home," said Mini.

"So, we thought we should run after them," said Maxi.

"And that's when he yelled at us and said all those mean things to us," Mini pouted.

"My, my," said Mommi. "I just can't imagine Ruff and Tuff running home without offering to help pick up those things. They'll certainly never make friends with Mr. Middleberry that way!"

Mini and Maxi looked at each other. They knew exactly what Mommi was trying to tell them. Without saying a word, they ran from the door, with Ruff and Tuff behind them.

42

Mr. Middleberry was still picking up some of his things when the four ran up. He looked tired, too.

"Stop! Stop!" said Maxi. "That's our job. Our pets knocked over your things, so we should pick them up."

"And we're so sorry about all this, too," said Mini.

Mr. Middleberry got up and tossed a pecan into the pecan basket. "I thought you might be back," he said. "So I saved a few things for you to pick up."

"Please forgive us," said Maxi. "We didn't mean to hurt you and The Tooti Frooti Shop."

"All right!" said Mr. Middleberry. "It's a deal. That is, if you forgive me for the mean things I said."

Before long The Tooti Frooti Shop was as good as new, except for the big red apples which Mr. Middleberry gave to Mini and Maxi. But you really do need something to eat while delivering a basket for Mr. Middleberry, don't you?

LET'S TALK ABOUT THIS

1. How did Maxi and Mini hurt Mr. Middleberry? How did he hurt them?
2. Why did they go back to The Tooti Frooti Shop with Ruff and Tuff?
3. What should we do when we hurt someone? What should we do when someone hurts us and is sorry about it? What would God want us to do about these things?

Philip—With Angels and Ethiopians

ACTS 8:4-8, 26-40

Philip was amazed to see what was happening. Wherever he went in Samaria, crowds came to hear him tell about Jesus. At a word from him, evil spirits went out of people, screaming as they left. Sick people were healed and lame people walked again.

It was clear that the power of God was working there through Philip. Everywhere, people were talking about the great joy they had in Jesus.

Certainly Philip was in the right place. And he was doing the right work for God.

But one day an angel came with a strange message. "God wants you to leave here," the angel said. "He wants you to go over to the road between Jerusalem and the Gaza Desert. You must get there about noon."

"Leave here?" Philip wondered. "Go there? Why?"

But the angel did not answer. Before Philip could say more the angel disappeared.

Philip could have stayed in Samaria. He could have kept on doing the great work he was doing.

But he didn't. God had told him to go somewhere else, so he went.

When Philip came to the Gaza Road, there was no one near. He looked this way and that, but there was not a person in sight.

"Why here?" Philip kept wondering. "Why leave all those people and come to this lonely place?"

Suddenly Philip saw a chariot coming in the distance. Who could it be?

"Go and run beside the chariot," the Holy Spirit told Philip.

Philip didn't stand there a second longer. He hurried over to the chariot and ran beside it.

Then Philip saw who was in the chariot. He was a very important man, the Treasurer of Ethiopia. He had been to the temple in Jerusalem to worship. Now he was on his way home, reading a scroll as he went.

"Do you know what you're reading?" Philip called to him.

"No," the man answered. "How can I? I need someone to explain it to me."

Then the Ethiopian asked Philip to come into the

chariot and tell him what it meant. Philip was so happy now. He could tell this important man about Jesus.

"He was led as a sheep to be killed," the Ethiopian read from the scroll. "He was quiet before those who were going to hurt Him."

Then the Ethiopian turned to Philip. "Was the Prophet Isaiah talking about himself?" he asked. "Or was he talking about someone else?"

Philip told the important man about the way Jesus had died for him. He told him what he could do to give his own life to Jesus.

"That is what I want to do," the man said.

Before long, Philip and the man came to a pool of water along the road. "Let's stop here," the man said. "I want you to baptize me."

"If you truly believe in Jesus, I will baptize you," said Philip.

"I do believe," said the man. "I believe that Jesus is God's Son."

So they stopped the chariot and went down into the water. By the side of the road, Philip baptized this important man from Ethiopia.

When they came out of the water, the Ethiopian turned to say "good-bye" to Philip. But Philip was gone. The Spirit of God had taken him away to some other place to do His work.

How happy this Ethiopian was to get back into his chariot and start toward home. He had so much to tell his friends there.

Of course, Philip never again wondered why God had sent him to this strange place. Through this one man, Philip had told hundreds of Ethiopians about Jesus, for the man in the chariot would tell many about Jesus.

Perhaps there was no other way for them to hear!

WHAT DO YOU THINK?
1. Why did God take Philip away from such important work in Samaria? Why did He send Philip to the lonely place on the Gaza Road?
2. What happened when Philip went to this strange place? Why was it so important for him to go there?
3. What do you think Philip learned from this?

That Dumb Donald Doolittle

"It's that dumb Donald Doolittle, that's who!" Mini shouted angrily. "He's the only one who would do that to Tuff!"

Maxi Muffin didn't say much as he untied the tin can from Tuff's tail. But he was sure that Mini was right. That little Donald Doolittle was the only boy in the neighborhood who would do that to Tuff.

"Yeah," said Maxi at last. "He's the one who put chewing gum in Ruff's hair the other day, too. I'm sure he was. I'd like to beat up on that little kid!"

"Love your enemies!" said Mommi, when Mini and Maxi told her about Ruff and Tuff. "Even Donald Doolittle."

"Dumb Donald?" asked Maxi. "Why should I love someone who sticks chewing gum in my dog's hair?"

"Or ties tin cans to my cat's tail?" added Mini.

"Because God wants you to!" Mommi said softly. "It may seem strange now, but when you do, you'll find that God knows best."

Mini and Maxi were still talking about loving Donald Doolittle as they went downtown for an ice cream cone. When they passed the tall board fence by Cherry Street, Mini suddenly grabbed Maxi's arm.

"Listen!" she whispered. "Isn't that a cat?"

"Sounds like it's hurt," said Maxi. "Must be on the other side of the fence."

Maxi and Mini ran to the end of the board fence. Then they tiptoed quietly along the row of bushes inside. As they came around a bush, they saw a boy, holding a cat on the ground while he tied a tin can to its tail.

"YOU DUMB DONALD DOOLITTLE!" Maxi and Mini both shouted.

Donald was so surprised that he jumped up. The cat jumped up, too, and let out a frightened YEOWWW and raced away with the can behind it.

"You dumb kid!" shouted Maxi. "Don't you know whose cat that is? That belongs to Chief Carter!"

"The Chief of POLICE???" Donald's eyes grew as big as saucers. "You won't tell him, willya, huh?"

"Why shouldn't we?" asked Maxi angrily. "You've been putting gum in Ruff's hair and tying cans to Tuff's tail. It would teach you a lesson. Maybe you wouldn't be such a mean little kid then."

Donald Doolittle started to cry. He really didn't look mean at all now. Maxi and Mini felt sorry for him.

"Love your enemies!" Mini whispered to Maxi.

"Even Donald Doolittle!" Maxi whispered back.

Then Maxi spoke softly to Donald. "We're going down to the ice cream shop," he said. "Come on and we'll buy you an ice cream cone."

"Me?" Donald asked. "Why me?"

"Because we want to be your friends," said Mini. "Jesus loves you, so we should, too."

Maxi and Mini got Donald a big ice cream cone. Then the three of them went to a little table outside to eat.

Who should come along just then but Chief Carter. When he saw Maxi and Mini, he came over to say hello.

"Who's your friend?" Chief Carter asked.

"Donald Doolittle," said Maxi. He almost said dumb Donald Doolittle, but he remembered what Mommi had said about loving his enemies.

"Donald Doolittle?" The chief frowned when he said that. "I've had some complaints around town about this boy. Seems he's been causing trouble. But if he's really your friend, then I may not have to keep my eye on him so much."

Donald wanted to hide under the table when the chief said that. Why didn't Maxi and Mini tell what he had done to the chief's cat?

As the chief started to leave, Donald jumped up. "Wait!" he shouted. "I have been causing trouble. I even tied a can to your cat's tail. But I will never, never do it again. I certainly don't want to hurt my new friends."

"Well, I'll be . . . ." said Chief Carter. "What happened to him?"

"Love your enemies," Maxi whispered to Mini.

"Even Donald Doolittle," Mini whispered back. "God was right, wasn't He?"

LET'S TALK ABOUT THIS

1. In the Bible story, what happened when Philip did what God told him to do, even though it may have seemed strange?

2. How were Maxi and Mini like Philip? What did they do that God wanted them to do, even though it may have seemed strange to them?

3. How might this story have ended if Maxi and Mini had not done what God wanted? How might Donald have been different?

4. Think of one thing you believe God wants you to do now. What may happen if you do it? What may happen if you don't?

Barnabas—
A True Friend

ACTS 9:26-31

Nobody wanted to be Saul's friend! Perhaps he wondered if anyone would ever be his friend again.

The Christians didn't want to be his friends. Why should they? Saul had gone about Jerusalem like a madman, killing Christians, throwing some in jail, and hurting others. No, the Christians were afraid of him.

Of course, the Christians in Jerusalem didn't know about the change in Saul's life. He had left Jerusalem an enemy of all Christians. But on the road to Damascus, he had talked with Jesus. Because of that, Saul had become a Christian.

Saul's old friends, who hated the Christians, had somehow learned about this. They had heard that Saul had given his life to Jesus, and they hated him for it. So they certainly did not want to be his friends now.

Saul was caught in the middle. His old friends hated him because he had become a Christian. And the Christians were afraid of him because of all that he had done to them. No, Saul didn't have a friend in the world. Or did he?

When Saul wanted a friend most, Barnabas came to help him.

Barnabas was everyone's friend. He loved other Christians so much that he had sold his land and had given the money to those who needed it. Of course, the Christians loved him. And they listened to him, too.

Barnabas may have been in Damascus when Saul met Jesus. He may have talked with Saul and learned about the way Saul became a new friend of Jesus. He was sure that Saul had come to love Jesus and wanted to live for Him now.

"Let's talk to the Christians in Jerusalem," Barnabas suggested to Saul.

"They surely must hate me," said Saul. "What will they do to me?"

But Barnabas took Saul to see the Jerusalem Christians anyway. And he told them all about Saul's trip to Damascus, and the way he had met Jesus along the way, and the way Saul was telling others about Jesus.

If Barnabas said these things, the Christians were sure that they were true. So they accepted Saul as one of them. Now Saul had many friends. All of Jesus' friends became his friends.

Saul also had some enemies. His old friends hated him more and more. Some of them made plans to kill him.

"You must leave here," Saul's new friends told him. "You must go away to another city."

Saul's Christian friends helped him go quietly from Jerusalem to Caesarea. From there, Saul went back to his hometown of Tarsus.

Saul must have wondered how he could do God's work by waiting in Tarsus. But he did wait. The Christians waited, too. They believed that Saul could do much for God later. But now his most important job was to wait.

While Saul waited for God to give him work to do, his new friends kept on working for Jesus. God helped them do many wonderful things. But they often prayed for Saul, and for the man who had been his true friend.

WHAT DO YOU THINK?
1. Why did Saul's old friends become his enemies? How did Saul find many new friends? Who helped him?
2. Who was Saul's true friend? How did he show that he was a true friend?

Maria

Nobody played with Maria during recess.

Nobody worked with Maria in the class projects.

And nobody talked with Maria after school. That is, nobody but Mini Muffin.

"Maria is different from the rest of us," some of them said.

"She even talks different," said others.

But Mini didn't care about those things. She thought that Maria and she could be friends.

"You're new in school, aren't you?" Mini asked.

"Yes," said Maria. "My home was in Mexico, so I do not talk well here."

"Well, I couldn't talk down there at all," said Mini. "How do you ever do it? I'm glad to have a friend like you."

Maria smiled. "And I'm glad to have a friend like you," she said.

"Then we should ask our mothers if you may come to my house to play this afternoon," said Mini.

Mini had so much fun with Maria. They played with dolls and games and Mini's stuffed animals.

"Now we should make something," said Mini. "But what should we make?"

"I know," said Maria. "We should make a pinata. It sounds like peen-YAH-ta. It is fun to make."

"A pinata?" asked Mini. "What is that?"

"We have fun with pinatas in Mexico," said Maria. "We fill a pinata with candy and little gifts. Then we break it with a stick. When the candy and gifts fall, we see who can pick up the most."

"Good!" said Mini. "Let's make a pinata."

Mini and Maria decided that they would make their first pinata without the candy and gifts. It wasn't easy to make one, but it was fun, even though their elephant did look more like a kangaroo turned upside down.

"What should we do with it?" Maria asked.

Mini Muffin thought for a moment. "Bring it to school tomorrow in a big bag," she said. "I have a plan."

The next day, Mini smiled as she saw Maria put her big paper bag by the coat rack. She was sure her plan would work.

When class started, the teacher stood at the front of the room. "Does anyone have something new for Show and Tell today?" she asked.

When Mini held up her hand, the teacher smiled. "What do you have, Mini?" she asked.

"I have nothing to show," said Mini. "But Maria does."

Twenty-three pair of eyes turned to stare at Maria. Maria wanted to hide.

But the teacher smiled and said, "Come up here, Maria, and tell us what you have brought."

Maria brought her big bag from the coat rack and took the pinata from it. Then she began to tell about her home in Mexico and the fun they had with pinatas. She wasn't afraid now. This was fun. The others were listening as though Maria were telling the most exciting story they had ever heard.

"May we have a pinata party?" Mini said when Maria had finished. "Maria could help us all make pinatas."

"Good!" said the teacher. "We will have our pinata party on Friday. Will you help us, Maria?"

When Friday came, Maria was the busiest girl in class. Everyone asked Maria to help with a pinata. Everyone talked to Maria when they could. And everyone played with Maria during recess.

"I have many friends now," Maria told Mini. "But you are my best friend. You are the best friend anyone could ever have."

"I have one more friend you should meet," said Mini. "He will be your very best friend."

"If he is your best friend, I want him to be my best friend, too," said Maria. "What is his name?"

"I will tell you about Him after school," said Mini. "His name is Jesus."

LET'S TALK ABOUT THIS

1. Why did Maria think that Mini was her best friend? What had Mini done to show that she was a true friend?

2. In what way was Mini like Barnabas?

3. What do you think Mini said to Maria after school? What do you tell your friends about Jesus? What should you tell them? Will you?

Dorcas—The Woman With Busy Hands

ACTS 9:36-41

"Who has the busiest hands in all Joppa?" people would ask.

"Dorcas, of course," was the answer.

Dorcas wasn't really her name. It was Tabitha. But people liked to call her Dorcas, which meant antelope, because she was always running to help other people.

Dorcas was so busy doing things for others that she never had time to do things for herself. Everyone loved this woman with the busy hands. Why shouldn't they?

"When my little girl was sick, who do you think was the first one there?" a mother said.

"Yes, and did you see the lovely clothes she made for us?" said another.

If Dorcas wasn't nursing sick people or making clothes for poor people, she was taking food to someone who didn't have any, or helping an older friend clean her house.

In all Joppa, there was no one like Dorcas.

In all Joppa, no one was loved more than Dorcas!

But one day, something sad happened. Nobody could believe it!

"Have you heard?" someone whispered. "Have you heard about Dorcas?"

"Don't tell me!"

"Yes. The dear soul just worked too hard. She died suddenly this morning."

"No! Not Dorcas! What will we do without her?"

All of the people of Joppa began to wonder what they would do without Dorcas. Who would help them when they got sick? Who would bring food, or mend clothes, or help the widows clean their houses?

With sad hearts, some of the women prepared her body to be buried. "If only Peter could come to see us," they said. "He would understand what to say to us now."

Then someone had an idea. "Peter isn't far away. He's visiting at Lydda now. Perhaps some of the men could ask him to come here."

It was a good idea! So some of the men of Joppa set out immediately to find him. Before long, they came back with Peter.

What a sad collection of friends Peter found when he came into the house. It looked like all Joppa had come there to cry about Dorcas.

As soon as the people saw Peter, they began to tell him what Dorcas had done for them. Then they begged Peter to say something to help them.

"I want you all to step out of the room," Peter said.

This wasn't really what they had in mind. What was Peter doing to them?

When they had left, Peter knelt down beside Dorcas' body and talked to God about Dorcas and her friends. Then tenderly, he spoke.

"Dorcas, you may get up now!" he said.

Slowly Dorcas opened her eyes and saw Peter standing there beside her. But what was she doing, lying there when she had guests?

"Oh! I'm sorry!" she said. "I must have been sleeping. I must get up and get something for you to eat."

"Wait," Peter whispered. "You must come with me first."

Peter took Dorcas by the hand and led her downstairs where her friends were waiting. When the friends heard Peter coming down the stairs, they turned to look. They could hardly believe their eyes! There was Dorcas, alive and well, walking down the stairs with Peter. God had brought her back to live with them again.

There was never so much excitement in all Joppa! Never! Wherever people met, they talked about the wonderful thing that had happened to their Dorcas.

Dorcas thought it was wonderful, too. Now she could keep on helping all her friends in Joppa.

WHAT DO YOU THINK?
1. What kind of a person was Dorcas? Why do you think people loved her so much?
2. Why do you think Dorcas did all these good things for people? What did her busy hands say about her love for God? What did they say about her love for others?

Welcome Wagon

"Mommi! Poppi!" Mini Muffin shouted. "Some people are moving into the empty house down the street."

"Did you see a big moving truck?" asked Mommi.

"No," said Mini. "There is no big moving truck."

"No moving truck?" asked Poppi. "How can they move all their things without a moving truck?"

Mommi and Poppi were still talking about the new neighbors and the moving truck that wasn't when Maxi ran into the house. "Guess what?" he said, catching his breath. "I just came from the new neighbors. Their other house burned so they don't have much to move into this one."

"Oh!" said Mommi. "How sad!"

"So that's why they have no moving truck," said Poppi. "We must do something to help them. But what?"

"I know," said Mommi. "I'll call some of the ladies in the neighborhood. We'll have a shower for them. It will certainly help to have a few new things for their house."

While Mommi talked about her shower, Maxi and Mini went out in the yard. "What can we do, Maxi?" Mini wondered.

"I don't know," said Maxi. "But it can't be some dumb old shower. That's for girls!"

Maxi and Mini sat in the yard for a long time, trying to think of some way they could help the new neighbors. Suddenly Mini looked up at the car going by. There were some words painted on the side of the car.

"What's a Welcome Wagon?" Mini asked.

"Someone in there will go to see the new neighbors," Maxi answered. "They will take some things to them and say how nice it is to have them move in. So what's the big thing about that?"

"That's it!" said Mini. "That's what we can do. Let's fix up a Welcome Wagon for the children."

It was such a good idea that Maxi couldn't find a thing wrong with it. So he and Mini ran to the garage to get the little red wagon. Then Maxi put an orange crate in the wagon and hung a sign on it that said "Welcome Wagon."

"This will be fun!" said Mini. As soon as they told Mommi and Poppi about their idea, they started down the street.

'Give a toy to the Welcome Wagon!'' they said to
ch of their friends in the neighborhood. Then
ey told their friends about the new neighbor chil-
en who had no toys. So each friend gave a toy for
e Welcome Wagon to take to the new neighbor
ildren.

At last the orange crate on the Welcome Wagon
s filled with toys. There were stuffed animals
d games and trucks and all kinds of things.

When the new neighbor children opened their
or, they could hardly believe their eyes. ''Sur-
ise! Surprise!'' said Mini and Maxi. ''The Wel-
me Wagon has come with all kinds of good
ings for you!''

What fun it was to help the new neighbor chil-
en carry their toys into the house. And what fun
was to watch them have fun with the new toys.

''Just like Dorcas!'' said the new neighbor mother.
usy hands for Jesus and His friends!''

''Do you know about Dorcas?'' asked Maxi. ''And
e you Jesus' friends?''

''Of course!'' said the new neighbors.

''Will you come to visit our Sunday School and
urch?'' asked Mini.

''We would like to very much,'' said the new
ighbors. So they did!

LET'S TALK ABOUT THIS

1. How were Maxi and Mini like Dorcas?
2. How can you be like Dorcas? Why should you be like
her?
3. Why would Jesus like to see you and your other
friends be like Dorcas?

63

RUTH—
THE GIRL WHO CAME TO BETHLEHEM

A Beautiful Girl of Moab

RUTH 1

"Our bread is almost gone," Naomi whispered to Elimelech. "What will we do?"

Elimelech shook his head sadly. "There is not much bread in all Bethlehem," he answered. "If only it would rain so that the wheat and barley would grow."

"But our sons," said Naomi. "They must have bread to eat."

"Then we must leave Bethlehem," said Elimelech. "We must go to a place where there is bread to eat."

"But where?" asked Naomi.

"Moab!" said Elimelech.

Naomi stared at Elimelech. "Moab! Do you want Mahlon and Chilion to grow up in Moab? Do you want them to marry Moabite girls?"

Elimelech thought for a moment. "It is better to

grow up in Moab than to starve in Bethlehem," he said.

So Naomi and Elimelech left for Moab. For a while, everything went well. There was more than enough bread. And the Moabites were really not so bad after all.

But one day Elimelech became very sick and died. Naomi was left alone in Moab with her two sons.

As time went by, Mahlon and Chilion married Moabite girls. Their names were Ruth and Orpah.

Then Mahlon died. Not long after that, Chilion died, too. Naomi now had no family with her except Ruth and Orpah.

"I must go back home to Bethlehem," Naomi said one day. "I cannot stay longer in Moab. This has been a sad place for me."

As Naomi made her way back toward Bethlehem, Ruth and Orpah walked with her. Before they had gone far, Naomi stopped to talk with them.

"You must not go back with me," she said. "I have nothing but a sad life to give you. Go back to your homes in Moab."

Orpah kissed Naomi and went back to her home. But Ruth would not return.

"Please don't ask me to leave you," said Ruth. "I want to go wherever you go. Where you live, I will live. Your people will be my people and your God

will be my God. As long as I live, I will stay with you, and even when I die, I will be buried with you."

Naomi smiled at Ruth. What a wonderful girl she was! There was not a finer girl in all of Israel. More than ever before, Naomi was happy that this Moabite girl loved her so much that she would give up everything for her.

When Naomi and Ruth came walking along the road into Bethlehem, the people were gathering barley in the fields. As soon as they saw Naomi coming, they ran to meet her.

"Is it really you?" they asked. "Is this really Naomi?"

There were so many questions to ask after all these years. The people crowded around Naomi and Ruth.

"Yes, this is Naomi," she answered. "But I've had such a bitter life in Moab that you should call me Mara."

Naomi told her friends about Elimelech. And about Mahlon and Chilion. She told them about Orpah, who went back to live with her people. Then Naomi told them about the beautiful girl named Ruth, the girl who loved her so much that she would not leave her.

That night in Bethlehem there was much to talk about. Sometimes the people talked about Naomi and her troubles in Moab. But mostly they talked about the beautiful girl from Moab who loved Naomi so much that she gave up everything to come back to Bethlehem with her.

"Has any girl in all Israel shown more love than this?" some asked.

But no one tried to answer.

WHAT DO YOU THINK?
1. What makes you think that Ruth loved Naomi? What did she do to show her love to Naomi? How much did she give up to show her love?
2. How do you think Naomi felt toward Ruth when Ruth loved her so much?
3. How do you think God felt about this little family and the love they showed each other?

69

The Zeblion

What fun it was to visit Grandmommi's house. Of course the most fun of all was to talk with Grandmommi and to see all of the wonderful things that she had made.

The Muffin Family said "ooh" or "aah" when they saw the beautiful pillows and aprons and lacy things that Grandmommi showed them. They were sure that nobody else could make such beautiful things.

"Now I have something for Maxi," said Grandmommi.

Maxi's eyes almost popped when he saw the bright ski cap that Grandmommi held out for him. "Did you make this yourself?" Maxi asked.

"Every stitch of it!" said Grandmommi. "And if you'll step into the next room, I have something there for Mini."

When the Muffin Family saw what Grandmommi
had for Mini, they laughed and laughed. That was
certainly something new!

"What is it?" Mini asked.

"A Zeblion!" said Grandmommi.

"A WHAT?" asked Mini.

"A Zeblion. You know, part zebra, part lion."

Of course! Anyone could see that now. It had a
zebra's striped body and a lion's big bushy head.

"Go ahead, Mini," said Grandmommi. "Ride
him!"

Mini jumped on the Zeblion and pretended to
ride him on a safari through the jungle. Then she
rode on a big cattle ranch out west.

"Now you have two big animals," said Mommi
Muffin to Mini. "You will have to start a stuffed
zoo!"

Then Mommi Muffin told Grandmommi about the big tiger that she had given Mini the week before. "For making the best grades in her class," said Mommi. "We bought it at the toy store."

Mini rode her new Zeblion while the others sat down to talk. But Mini began to ride slower and slower.

"What's the matter, Mini?" asked Mommi. "You look sad. You shouldn't be sad when you have such a nice gift."

"But that's why I'm sad," said Mini.

"I don't understand," said Grandmommi. "Did I do something wrong?"

Mini ran over to Grandmommi and threw her arms around her. "No, Grandmommi," she said. "You were wonderful, and the Zeblion is wonderful. But I have two big animals. And my friend Maria doesn't have any. That's why I'm sad."

Grandmommi looked at Mommi Muffin and smiled. They both waited to hear what else Mini would say.

"I really want to give one of my big animals to Maria," she said.

"I think that would be a wonderful thing to do," said Mommi.

"So do I, Mini," said Grandmommi. "But which one will you give her?"

"You made the Zeblion for me," said Mini. "So I should not give that away. Would it be all right if I gave her my big tiger, Mommi?"

"Of course," said Mommi. "I know that will show how much you love Maria *and* Jesus."

LET'S TALK ABOUT THIS

1. In the Bible story, what did Ruth give up that showed how much she loved Naomi and God?

2. Why did Mini want to give one of her new stuffed animals?

3. Why did Mommi say, "that would be a wonderful thing to do"? How did this show that Mini loved Maria? How did it show that she loved Jesus?

73

In the Barley Fields of Bethlehem

RUTH 2

"Where are you going?" Naomi asked.

Ruth smiled sweetly. "To the barley fields to glean for us," she said.

In those days, poor people went behind the reapers who gathered the stalks of grain. They could keep all the grain that the reapers left behind. That was called gleaning.

"What a wonderful girl!" Naomi whispered to herself as Ruth walked toward the barley fields. "To think that she will glean for both of us."

Gleaning was hard work. It would not be easy for Naomi to do this all day for a little barley.

It wasn't easy for Ruth, either. She knew that some of the people might not like Moabites. They might not be happy to see a Moabite girl glean in their fields.

But Ruth went to glean anyway. How else could she find food for both herself and Naomi?

Ruth worked hard to gather the barley stalks. She did not notice an important man come into the fields where she was working. She did not hear this man talking with the servant in charge of the field.

"Who is the young woman over there?" the man asked the servant.

"Ruth, the Moabitess, who came here to live with Naomi," the servant answered. "She asked if she could glean here for herself and Naomi. She has been working all day."

The man walked over to Ruth. He watched her working busily to gather the barley stalks.

Suddenly Ruth looked up. She was surprised to see this man watching her.

"Oh!" she said. "I'm sorry. I did not see you."

"My name is Boaz," said the man. "This field belongs to me."

Ruth wondered what Boaz would say to her. Would he make her leave his field? Would he be angry because a Moabite was gleaning in his field?

"Stay here in my field," Boaz said. "I have told my people to share their water with you. They will not hurt you."

Ruth bowed down before Boaz to thank him. "Why are you being so kind to a Moabite girl?" she asked.

"Because you have been so kind to Naomi," he

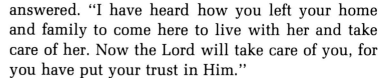

answered. "I have heard how you left your home and family to come here to live with her and take care of her. Now the Lord will take care of you, for you have put your trust in Him."

Ruth smiled at Boaz. "Thank you for being so friendly to me, even though I am a Moabite," she said.

When it was noon, Boaz asked Ruth to eat with him and his reapers. He made sure that Ruth had all that she wanted to eat, too.

"Break some stalks of barley and leave them behind for Ruth to gather," he told the reapers. "Don't say anything about it, either!"

When evening came, Ruth beat the grains of barley from the stalks. She was surprised to see that she had almost a bushel of grain.

"Where did you get all that?" Naomi asked when Ruth brought it home.

Ruth was so happy to tell Naomi about the kind man who had become her friend. "His name is Boaz!" she said.

"Boaz!" Naomi whispered. "He is one of the closest members of our family!"

"He told me to come back," said Ruth. "He said I could work with his reapers until they are finished."

Naomi was so happy. "Then you should do it," she said.

So Ruth worked in the fields of Boaz until the reapers were finished. Each day she brought home

76

the barley she had gathered and shared it with Naomi. Each day Ruth and Naomi talked about Boaz, the kind man who was helping them so much.

"God has been good to send such a wonderful friend," they would often say. "We must remember to thank Him for Boaz."

So they did!

WHAT DO YOU THINK?
1. How did Ruth help to take care of Naomi? How did Boaz help to take care of Naomi and Ruth? How did God help Boaz do this?
2. How do you think Naomi felt about Ruth and her kindness? How do you think she and Ruth felt about Boaz and his kindness? Do you think there was much love in this family?
3. How do you think God felt about the people in this family and the way they helped each other?

Surprise Boxes

"Surprise!" said Grandmommi. "Inside these four boxes you will find four surprises. I think you'll have fun with your surprises. If you use them well, they will help you in many ways."

"Whatever can they be?" Mommi wondered.

"Mittens!" said Mini.

"In the middle of summer?" said Maxi. "I think they're handkerchiefs."

"Let me give you some clues," said Grandmommi. "Then you may guess. The first clue is something like a sweet roll."

The Muffin Family looked at one another. They looked puzzled. "A sweet roll?" they all said.

"Donut?" said Maxi slowly.

Grandmommi shook her head.

"Cinnamon roll? Long John? Hot cross buns?" Mommi wondered aloud.

"No, none of those," said Grandmommi.

"Corn bread?" asked Poppi with a chuckle.

"Muffin!" chimed Mini. "That's us!"

Grandmommi clapped her hands. "You're right, Mini," she said. "Now for the second clue." Grandmommi rocked her arms as if she were holding a baby.

"Baby?" Mommi asked. "Cradle?"

"Doll?" asked Maxi.

"Maxi guessed it!" said Grandmommi. "Time to open your packages now."

78

The Muffin Family looked more puzzled than ever now as each opened a package. "Muffin? Doll? I don't get it!" said Poppi.

"Oh! Oh! Look at this!" Mini almost shouted as she held up a little Mini Muffin rag doll. It looked just like her.

The others found rag dolls that looked just like them, too. What a surprise!

"And to think that you made them!" said Mommi. "They are so cute."

"Useful, too," said Grandmommi.

"I don't understand," said Poppi.

"These rag dolls can tell stories," said Grandmommi. "They can say things to each other that the real Muffin Family may not say. And they will help you learn lessons from one another, too."

"Muffin Family stories!" said Mommi. "How wonderful! We'll do it."

At first, each person took his own doll. Maxi talked for the Maxi doll. Mini talked for the Mini doll.

The Muffin Family's rag doll family *was* fun. Grandmommi was right.

Then the real Muffin Family traded dolls for another story. Poppi talked for the Mommi doll. Mommi talked for the Poppi doll. Mini and Maxi traded, too.

You should have heard Maxi trying to say the things that Mini would say! And Poppi learned a thing or two trying to talk like Mommi.

"These rag dolls really can do some great things for our family," said Poppi. "That was very kind of you to make them for us."

"Yes," said Mommi, "I know they will help us to understand each other better."

"When you do," said Grandmommi, "you will know how you can all please the Lord more. I'll be praying that they will help you all."

Maxi lifted his Maxi doll and made it bow to Grandmommi. "I'll make sure they do!" he said.

"I'll shake to that!" said Grandmommi. She reached out her hand and shook hands with the Maxi doll.

The Muffin Family laughed at this. That is, the *real* Muffin Family. They all prayed together that their Muffin Family dolls would help them as a family.

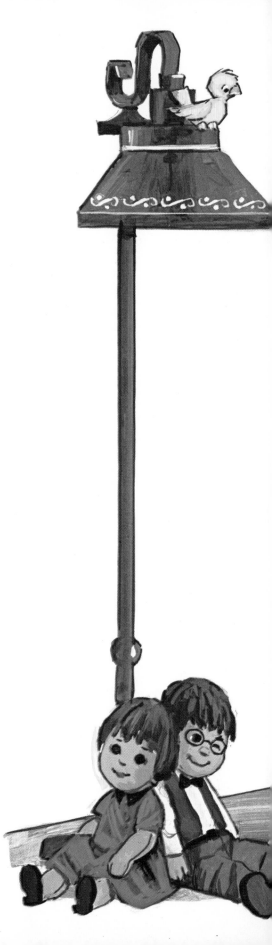

LET'S TALK ABOUT THIS

1. In the Bible story, how did Ruth show kindness to Naomi?

2. How did Grandmommi show kindness to her family in this story? What did she do for her family that was better than just making a gift for them?

3. Think of some ways you can show kindness to your family. What can you do tomorrow? Will you? How could the Muffin Family rag dolls help you and your family to talk about some family problems? What would you want them to change? Can you and your family talk about ways to solve these problems now? Will you?

Bethlehem's Happy Family

RUTH 3—4

Each day Ruth went into the fields to work. She gathered grain for herself and Naomi. Each day Naomi thought about this wonderful girl who took care of her.

"Don't you think you should get married again?" Naomi asked Ruth one day.

Ruth smiled and blushed. Of course she would like to get married. But to whom?

"To Boaz!" said Naomi. "Look at all that he's done for you. He would like to marry you, I'm sure, but he probably thinks that he's too old for you."

"He's a wonderful man," whispered Ruth. "He would make such a good husband!"

"Then get dressed in your best clothes," said Naomi. "Put on some perfume and go down to the threshing floor where Boaz is working. Then do exactly what I tell you."

Ruth listened carefully as Naomi told about her plan. "Wait until he has finished eating and lies down to sleep tonight," said Naomi. "Then lie down quietly at his feet until he wakes up."

So Ruth did exactly as Naomi said. When Boaz had finished eating, he lay down by a heap of barley and went to sleep. Then Ruth went quietly over, lay down at his feet, and covered herself.

Boaz woke up suddenly about midnight and saw someone lying at his feet. Surprised by this, he sat up straight.

"Who's there?" he asked.

"It's Ruth," she whispered.

Then Ruth told Boaz why she had come to see him. "You are one of the closest persons in Naomi's family," she said. "According to Jewish law, you could marry me so that Naomi could have a grandchild."

"What a wonderful girl you are!" Boaz said. "May the Lord richly bless you! This is one of the kindest things you have ever done for Naomi. I know that you would rather marry a young man, but you're willing to marry me, an older man, so that Naomi can have grandchildren."

Then Boaz made a promise to Ruth. "There is one man who is closer to Naomi's family than I am," he said. "Tomorrow I will talk with him. If he wants to marry you, then he is first. But if he doesn't, I'll take care of everything. Now go to sleep, and I'll talk with this man in the morning."

So Ruth slept that night at the feet of Boaz. Very early the next morning, before the sun came up, she got up to go home.

"Take this barley home as a gift to Naomi," said Boaz. Then he poured about a bushel and a half of barley into Ruth's shawl, tied it up and sent it home with her.

Of course, Naomi was excited to see Ruth come home. "What happened?" she asked. "Tell me everything."

So Ruth told Naomi all that had happened. Then she gave Naomi the barley that Boaz had sent.

"Boaz will do everything he said," Naomi promised. "Wait and see!"

Sure enough, the next morning, Boaz went into town to look for the other relative. "There you are," he said when he had found him. "We need to talk about something important."

When people talked about important things in those days, they asked some other people to listen. Boaz asked ten men to hear what he had to say.

Boaz and the other man sat down in the marketplace to talk. "Naomi is selling all that belonged to Elimelech and her two sons," said Boaz. "Would you like to buy them?"

"Of course," said the other man.

"You must also marry Ruth," said Boaz. "That's part of the deal."

"Then I can't buy Elimelech's things," said the other man. "I don't want any children Ruth may have to get the things that are already mine. No, Boaz, you may buy these things and marry Ruth."

When people decided to do something like that, they had a strange way to show that it was a promise. The man pulled off his sandal and gave it to Boaz.

Then Boaz talked to the ten men around them. "You all know now that I am buying Elimelech's things and that I will marry Ruth."

"Yes, we know," they said. "We hope you will have many children and will become rich."

Boaz did marry Ruth as he had promised. As time went by, God sent a baby boy into their home. Boaz and Ruth named him Obed.

The women of Bethlehem were so happy about this new baby that they came to see Naomi. "This baby may grow up to become famous!" they said.

The women were right! The little baby did grow up to become famous. Years later, he would become the grandfather of the great King David.

Boaz and Ruth were very happy for the new baby that God sent. And they were very, very happy for all the wonderful things that God had done in their family.

WHAT DO YOU THINK?
1. Who did Ruth try to please most? How did this help Ruth to find someone who would make her a happy wife and mother?
2. What had Boaz done to cause Ruth to love him? What had Ruth done to cause Boaz to love her? How might their love for each other have changed if they had each been selfish?
3. How might this story have been different if Naomi had been a selfish person? If Ruth had been a selfish person? If Boaz had been a selfish person?

Picnic Plans
and Alphabet Problems

It was always fun to plan a picnic. But why couldn't Mini and Maxi ever agree on things like that?

"Let's go to the beach," said Maxi.

"No, let's go to the park," said Mini.

Mommi and Poppi Muffin didn't quite know how they could go to both places at once. No, Mini and Maxi would have to do better than that.

"But I want to run in the sand," said Maxi.

"And I want to swing on the swings with my friends," said Mini.

Poppi winked at Mommi.

Mommi smiled at Poppi.

"I think we have alphabet problems," said Poppi.

"Alphabet problems?" asked Mini and Maxi. "What are those?"

"Too much I. Not enough U," said Poppi. "Mini is thinking about what Mini wants, and Maxi is thinking about what Maxi wants."

Maxi and Mini both hung their heads. They knew that Poppi was right. They *had* been thinking too much about themselves.

"Perhaps it's time for the Muffin Family rag dolls that Grandmommi gave us," said Mommi.

When Mommi came back with the Maxi and Mini rag dolls, she held them out. "Who would like to do some pretending?" she asked.

"I will," said Mini. "That should be fun."

Mini took the two rag dolls and held them up for all to see. "Now, where shall we go for our picnic?" asked the real Mini.

"To the beach!" shouted the Maxi rag doll.

"To the park!" shouted the Mini rag doll.

"Dumb girl! You always get your way!" grumbled the Maxi doll.

"Not this time," said the Mini doll. "If you want to go to the beach, I'll go."

When the real Maxi heard that, he didn't wait for Mini to go on with her rag doll talk. "Aw, come on," he said. "You don't have to be a hero. I'll go to the park if you want to go there."

"Quiet!" said Mini. "The Mini and Maxi rag dolls are still talking."

Then Mini went on talking through the rag dolls. "Aw, come on," said the Maxi doll. "You don't have to be a hero. I'll go to the park if you want to go there."

"I have a better idea," said the Mini doll. "Let's go to the park in the morning. Then we will have our picnic lunch on the beach and stay there in the afternoon!"

"That's a great idea," said the Maxi doll. "I'm glad that I thought of it."

"But I didn't," said the real Maxi. "You did."

Mini looked stern. "Will the audience please stop interrupting!" she said.

"But I think it's a great idea," said the real Maxi. "Even if you did think of it."

"Seems that we may have solved our alphabet problems," said Poppi.

"And our picnic problems!" said Mommi. "Now let's all help to pack the picnic lunch!"

So they did. Even the Mini and Maxi dolls did their part, and they didn't grumble a bit.

LET'S TALK ABOUT THIS

1. What did Poppi mean when he said "alphabet problems"? In the Bible story, did Ruth and her family put the "I" first or the "U" first?

2. How did the Mini and Maxi rag dolls help the Muffin Family solve their alphabet problems?

3. What do you think God wants you to do about your alphabet problems? In what ways do you have too much I and not enough U? How can you change this to please God more?

STORIES
THAT JESUS TOLD

The Fool

LUKE 12:13-34

Jesus told a story one day about a rich fool. Here is what He said.

Once there was a man who had everything. He had big fields of grain. He had big barns that were filled. He had houses and things. Yes, this man had everything.

But he was a fool. God said so!

"Look what I have," the man would say to himself. "I have big barns filled with grain. But I must have more! I'll tear down my big barns and make bigger barns. I'll fill them with more grain. If the bigger barns aren't big enough, I'll tear those down and make still bigger ones."

The man who had everything never thought about God. Why should he? He didn't need God. He already had everything. What more could God give him?

Of course, the man was really a fool. That's what God called him.

The man who had everything never thought much about others, either. Why did he need a family? What would friends do for him? They would just take some of his money away from him. That's all. No! He certainly didn't want to bother with friends or family.

So the man who had everything spent his time looking at all the things he had. He counted his money and bragged to himself about all his things.

But he never gave any of it away.

And he never shared anything with others.

And of course he never used any of it for God.

That's why he was a fool. That's why God told him that he was.

"You fool!" God said one day. "You will never live to see tomorrow's sunrise."

Sunrise? The man had never bothered to think about the sunrise. But now he was terrified. He would give anything to see the sunrise again.

God wasn't angry because the man had money. He was angry because the man loved his money more than God or others.

"Tonight you will die!" God told the man. "But you cannot take your money with you."

Somehow the man had always thought that he would take his money with him. But who would get it now? And if he didn't take his money along, he would be poor wherever he was going!

"Wait!" the man cried out in panic. "Let me pay You to help me! My servants will steal it all when they find me dead in the morning!"

But it was too late. The richest man in the land suddenly became the poorest, for he left every coin behind as he died.

Yes, the man was a fool. God said so! He had everything. But he really had nothing.

WHAT DO YOU THINK?

1. Why was God not pleased with this man? Why did God call him a fool?

2. Why was the man who had everything actually a man who had nothing?

3. How would this story have changed if the man had loved God and others?

Mine!

"That's MINE!" said Maxi.

"But I only wanted to look at your new book, Maxi," said Mini.

"I don't care," said Maxi. "It's MINE!"

Things had gone that way all day. When Mini had asked to listen to one of his records, Maxi had said, "No, it's MINE!" When she had picked up Maxi's cap from the floor, he said it again. "MINE! I'll get it!"

"Maxi," said Poppi Muffin, "that must be at least a dozen times I've heard you say MINE since I came home. Sounds like you own the world."

"But my things are MINE," said Maxi. "Why doesn't Mini stop bugging me?"

Poppi thought for a moment. "Hmmm," he said. "What would you think if God said that about all His things when you want to share them?"

"What things?" Maxi asked.

"Oh, such little things as sunshine, the clouds, the blue sky, the green grass, and a few hundred others," said Poppi. "Why don't you think about that a little?"

94

Maxi was quiet the rest of the evening. Poppi was sure that Maxi must be thinking about the things he had said.

That night Maxi tossed and turned. He kicked the covers from his bed and tried to cover himself with his pillow. By morning, Maxi and his covers and pillow looked like a bowl of spaghetti on the floor.

"You look tired, Maxi," said Poppi at breakfast. "Didn't you sleep well?"

"No," said Maxi. "I had bad dreams."

Just then Mini thought of something. "Oh, Maxi," she said. "I have to take something about the sea to school today. May I take one of your seashells?"

"Sure, Mini," said Maxi. "You can take more if you want."

Poppi almost dropped his coffee cup.

And Mommi almost poured the cream in Poppi's lap. They were sure that Maxi would say MINE.

"Why don't you show them the driftwood I picked up at the beach, too?" Maxi asked.

Mommi looked at Poppi. Poppi looked at Mommi. Something *had* happened to Maxi.

"Why the big switch?" asked Poppi. "Last night everything was MINE! This morning you're giving the world away. Would you like to tell us something?"

"Well," said Maxi. Maxi figured that was a safe way to begin when he wasn't sure what to say next. Nobody could argue with that!

96

"It was my dream last night," Maxi went on. "First I went down to the beach to play on the sand. But God said MINE and pulled all the beach away. I tried to swim, but God said MINE again and pulled the water away."

Maxi looked around. Everyone was listening to him as though he were a favorite TV program.

"Every time I tried to do something, God took His things away from me," said Maxi. "Then when I tried to lie out in the sunshine, God pulled the sun away and said MINE again. It was dark and cold and . . . and . . ."

"And what?" asked Poppi.

"And then I woke up on the floor without any covers on me," said Maxi.

"Do you want to tell us something else?" asked Poppi.

"Well," said Maxi again. "I figured that if God did what I had been doing, the world would be a terrible place. I guess He shares all His things here with me, so I should share my things with Mini, and with Him."

"Then you didn't have bad dreams," said Poppi. "Those were good dreams, for they helped you do good things that please God."

LET'S TALK ABOUT THIS

1. How was Maxi like the man in the Bible story at first? Do you think that man may have said MINE to the people around him?

2. What could happen if God said MINE whenever we wanted to share His good gifts?

3. In what ways does God want us to share our things with Him? In what ways does He want us to share them with others?

97

The Boy Who Came Home

LUKE 15:11-32

There was once a father who had two sons. The father loved both of his sons, even though they were quite different.

One son worked hard for his father and tried to please him. But the other son didn't. He never cared much for the way others felt, even his father.

One day this thoughtless son had an idea. So he went to see his father about it.

"When you die, my brother and I will get what you have," he said. "Why don't you give my part to me now so I can do what I want with it."

What a thoughtless thing to say to his father! But this young man didn't care. It didn't matter how sad his father felt about this.

Of course, the father didn't want to do this. But he was a very kind man and wanted the best for his son.

"Perhaps he will be happier if he can have his own money," the father thought. "Perhaps he will find a wise way to use it."

But the son certainly wasn't thinking about a way to use this money. He was thinking of the fun he would have spending it.

98

"This will be great fun," he thought as he went far from home. So he spent the money on parties and friends. When people heard that he had money to spend, he had many friends, too.

One day the young man found that his money was gone. He had spent it all. Now he had nothing, not even enough to buy food.

"What will I do?" he thought. "Perhaps my friends will give me something to eat."

But when the young man's friends found that he had no more money, they didn't even want to see him. And they certainly didn't want to share their food with him.

Things became worse, too, for a famine came upon the land. Nobody had much food to eat. The young man was so afraid now. How he wished he had some of his money back again! But he didn't.

The foolish son didn't want to work, but he knew that he must. But what could he do? He had never learned to do any kind of work. So the best job he could find was to take care of pigs.

The young man became more and more hungry. At times he thought he should eat some of the food that was given to the pigs.

Often this foolish young man would dream of

home and his family. They certainly had plenty of food to eat. Even the servants had more than enough.

The more he thought of home, the more he realized what a good home and family he had. And the more he knew what a foolish young man he had been!

"If only I could go back," he thought. "I would even be willing to be a servant."

At last the young man decided that he would go back. And he would ask his father to forgive him and make him a servant.

By this time, the father was afraid that his son had died. He had heard nothing from him since he had left. Often he would sit by the road and long for his son to come home.

Then one day the father saw his son coming down the road. But he was not the proud young man who had gone away. He was a dirty young man with ragged clothes. But the father didn't care. This was still his son. So he ran and threw his arms around him.

"Father, I have sinned against heaven and you,"

the young man began. "Let me come home as a servant."

The father was so happy to see his son! Then he called to his servants. "Give him the best robe and bring him the best food that we have. My son was lost, but now he is found. I thought he was dead, but now he's alive."

Jesus' story was really about His Father in heaven, happy to welcome any lost person who comes, asking for forgiveness. When a lost person comes to God and wants to be forgiven, He is happy to receive him as a father receives a lost child.

WHAT DO YOU THINK?
1. What does this story tell about people who come to God, asking to be forgiven? What does it say about the way God receives them?
2. Why do you think God receives people who have done so many things to hurt Him? Why doesn't He tell them to go away?
3. What if the son had never come to ask for the father's forgiveness? How would this story have been different?
4. What if the father had not been willing to forgive the son? How would this story have been different?

One of Those Days!

Now and then we all have a bad day. Even Mini Muffin. But Mini found that bad days often seem to get worse.

It was one of those bad days when Mini caught her finger in her bedroom door. To make matters worse, she kicked the door as hard as she could and left a big scuff mark on the door.

"Mini!" Mommi scolded. "What should I do with you?"

"Spank her!" said Maxi.

Mini wanted to say a few things that little girls shouldn't say to their big brothers, but she decided that Maxi might say a few things that big brothers shouldn't say to their little sisters. So she didn't.

Mini's bad day got worse when she sat down in a big huff in the family-room chair. The problem was that Tuff had been there first and Mini didn't see her.

Tuff let out a YEOWWWW that sounded like an Apache war cry, then jumped across the table, knocking over a vase of flowers. By the time Mommi and Maxi got into the room, the water from the vase was running across the floor and onto the rug.

"Mini Muffin!" said Mommi. "What should I do with you?"

"Spank her!" said Maxi.

Mini was too angry to say anything, so she ran through the back door and slammed the screen door behind her. But the problem was that Ruff was running behind her. He got through before she slammed the screen door, but his tail didn't.

"YIIIIK, YIIIIK," Ruff cried, and began chasing his wounded tail round and round.

"MINI!" Mommi almost shouted when she said that, as much as mothers should shout when they have something to say to their little girls. "What AM I going to do with you?"

"Spank her!" Maxi said again.

But just as Maxi said that, he stepped back and plopped his foot on Ruff's wounded tail. It seems that Ruff had come up behind Maxi to lie down.

"YIIIIK, YIIIIK," Ruff cried again, and began chasing his wounded tail round and round.

"MAXI," Mommi said. "Now what am I going to do with you?"

Mini Muffin wanted to say "spank him," but she didn't. Instead, she said, "Love him."

Maxi felt sorry when he heard Mini say that. He picked up Ruff for some comfort and went toward the door. But Maxi couldn't see through Ruff's tail, which swished back and forth across his face like a windshield wiper. He stepped on some marbles he had left on the floor and went sailing across the room, dropping Ruff neatly into the aquarium.

Just then Poppi Muffin walked into the room. "I don't believe it!" he said quietly. "I really don't believe it!" Maxi didn't believe it either, especially as he sat there on some marbles, with Ruff shaking his wet fur all over him.

"MAXI MUFFIN!" Mommi shouted. "You can just clean up all this mess. You should be ashamed of yourself."

"I'll help you, Maxi," said Mini.

Poppi Muffin stood there scratching his head as Mini helped Maxi clean up the mess. "Why?" he asked. "Why is she doing that?"

"Blessed are those who forgive!" Mommi whispered. "What do you think of that?"

"I think it's wonderful, even though I don't remember those exact words in the Bible!" said Poppi. "Let's go take a walk with Ruff and Tuff while they clean up!"

LET'S TALK ABOUT THIS

1. In the Bible story, how did the father feel about the boy who had hurt him? How did the boy's brother feel about him?

2. Why do you think Mini showed love to Maxi when he had been telling Mommi to spank her? Was she more like the father or the brother in the Bible story?

3. Think of some people who have hurt you. What can you do to show that you have forgiven them? What have you done?

Jesus was always having problems with the Pharisees. They didn't like Jesus because He said He was God's Son. They thought He was just another man. So they didn't listen to many of the things He told them about God and heaven.

One day Jesus told them a story. It was a story about a father and his two sons. But it was really a story about the Pharisees. Here is the way Jesus' story went:

A Story About Yes and No

MATTHEW 21:28-32

One morning a father got ready to work in his vineyard. "Will you help me?" he asked one of his sons.

"No," said the son. "I want to have some fun with my friends."

The father was so sad as he watched his son go away. He was sorry that his son said no when he needed help.

About that time, the father's other son came along. "How about you?" the father asked. "Will you help me in the vineyard today?"

"Yes," said the second son. "I'll be glad to help you in the vineyard."

Now that was what the father wanted to hear from his sons. He was so happy! Why couldn't his other son be like that?

The father thought about his sons as he went into the storehouse to get some baskets. But when he came out, he was certainly surprised.

There stood the son who had said no.

The son who had said yes was gone.

"Where is your brother?" the father asked. "He was going to help me in the vineyard."

"He went away to have fun with his friends," said the first son.

"But you said you were going away," said the father.

"I know," said the first son. "But I began to see how wrong that was. I'm sorry. I've come back to help you in the vineyard today."

The father was very happy to hear this.

But he was very sad to hear about his other son.

The son who said no at first really said yes. But the son who said yes at first really said no.

Jesus began to talk with the Pharisees about His story.

"Which of the two sons obeyed his father?" He asked.

"The first son," they answered.

"But you are like the second son," Jesus told them. "You promised God to obey Him. Yet you won't listen to those He has sent. You won't turn away from your sin and ask God to forgive you. Even the tax collectors and sinners do that! So they will get to heaven instead of you."

The Pharisees were very angry when Jesus said this. How dare He say that tax collectors and sinners would get to heaven instead of them!

But Jesus knew all about heaven. Why shouldn't He? It's His home, isn't it?

WHAT DO YOU THINK?
1. Which son obeyed his father in this story? Why?
2. Which son was like the Pharisees? What were they doing that was wrong? What were some tax collectors and sinners doing that was better? Why was it better?
3. Would God rather have people say no at first, but then obey, or to say yes at first, but not obey?

Who's Sitting in My Chair?

"Poppi!" said Maxi, as soon as Poppi walked through the door. "Guess what Ruff can do now?"

"Stand on his head?" asked Poppi with a grin. "Wiggle his ears?"

"No, of course not," said Maxi. "But come and see what he can do."

Poppi was always glad to see new things that had happened at home during the day. So he said hello to Mommi and went to the back yard with Maxi.

"OK, you stay here," said Maxi. "And Ruff, you come over here." Ruff went with Maxi exactly where Maxi said.

"Now sit!" Maxi said to Ruff. Without waiting a moment, Ruff sat.

"OK, now STAY!" Maxi ordered. Then Maxi ran across the yard. Ruff almost got up, but he didn't.

"Very good," said Poppi. "Ruff's learning to obey."

"That's what I want," said Maxi. "Any dog of mine is going to obey or else!"

"Or else what?" asked Poppi with a grin.

"Well, just *or else*," said Maxi.

Poppi went inside while Maxi stayed out to play with Ruff. It didn't seem long at all until Mommi opened the door and called to Maxi. "Dinner!" she said. "Come quickly!"

"OK," said Maxi. "Coming!"

Mommi put the dinner on the table. Everyone sat down to eat. That is, everyone but Maxi.

"Where IS that boy?" asked Mommi. "We're all waiting." So Mommi opened the door again and called to Maxi.

"Maxi!" she said. "Will you please come. We're all waiting at the table."

Maxi was having so much fun with Ruff. It was easy to see that. "Coming!" he called back.

Mommi went back to the table. She sat down with Poppi and Mini. They waited and waited, but Maxi still did not come.

"This time, you call him," said Mommi. "Our food is getting cold."

Poppi opened the back door. Maxi was still play-ing with Ruff. He started to call for Maxi. But then he had another idea.

"Here, Ruff! Come here, boy!" he called.

Ruff came running across the lawn as fast as he could go. Then he and Poppi went into the house.

When Maxi washed and came into the room to eat, imagine his surprise! There was Ruff, sitting in his chair, puffing happily. Everyone else was eating dinner.

"Hey! What's that dumb dog doing in my chair?" asked Maxi.

"He's not so dumb," said Poppi. "He knows when to come for dinner. He's smart enough to know that it pays to obey!"

And Maxi was smart enough to know what Poppi meant. Hadn't he just said that any dog of his was going to obey *or else*?

"I . . . I did say that I was coming," Maxi said weakly.

"Hmmm," said Poppi. "Ruff didn't say a word. He just obeyed. I'll let you decide which is better, Maxi. And while you're deciding, tell Ruff to get off your chair so you can eat."

Of course, Ruff obeyed. And Maxi did too, whenever he could remember.

LET'S TALK ABOUT THIS
1. Who obeyed better, Ruff or Maxi? Why?
2. Which boy in the Bible story was Ruff like? Which one was Maxi like at first?
3. Do you sometimes say you will do something instead of doing it? How can you change that to please your parents more? How can you change it to please God more?

Talents and Treasures

MATTHEW 25:14-30

For months now Jesus had been training His twelve disciples to do His work. But what would they do with all this talent when He went back to heaven?

Jesus told this story to help them know what they should do while He was gone.

There was once a man who planned to go away for a long time. Before he left, he talked with three of his servants and asked them to take care of his things while he was gone.

"I must trust you to do well with my treasures," he said. "Use them wisely."

Then he gave one servant five pieces of gold. "Use these well for me while I am gone," he said.

To another servant he gave two pieces of gold. "Use these well for me while I am gone," he told this servant.

And to a third servant he gave one piece of gold. "You also must use this well for me while I am gone."

As soon as the master went away, the first servant began to work. He went to the markets and bought some things. Then he traded them for better things. At last he sold these for more than he had paid.

The second servant did the same. He went each day to the market. He also bought some things and traded them for better things. Then he sold them for more than he had paid.

But the third servant was lazy. He laughed at the other two servants for working so hard.

"Look at them!" he often said. "While I'm having fun, they're off somewhere trying to make my rich master richer!"

One day the lazy servant was sleeping when he heard some other servants shouting. "The master is home! The master is home!"

Quickly he jumped up. He knew now that he had done nothing with the master's gold. What could he do?

But it was too late. Another servant pounded on his door. "The master wants to see you," he shouted. "NOW!"

The lazy servant picked up the one piece of gold and ran to meet the master. He wondered what the master would say.

"How well have you used my treasure?" the master asked the three servants.

"I have used your five gold pieces to earn five more," said the first servant. "Now I have ten for you."

"Good work!" said the master. "And I have something for you, too. You will have the best job that I can give you. Now I know that I can trust you with anything."

Then the second servant stepped up. "You gave me two pieces of gold," he said. "I have earned two more for you. Here are the four!"

"Good work!" said the master. "I have a wonderful job for you, too. For now I know that I can trust you."

The other servants were jealous. These two would have great power and honor now. But they knew that the faithful servants had worked hard to earn it.

The third servant hung his head as he stepped up to meet the master. "I did nothing with your gold piece," he said, "so I have nothing more to give you."

"You lazy, good-for-nothing servant," the master shouted. "Didn't you even take it to the bankers and let them use it for me?"

Then the master gave orders to the other servants. "Take his piece of gold and give it to my most trusted servant," he said. "Then throw this lazy fellow out."

So the lazy servant went out with nothing. But the two servants whom the master could trust went to do their most important work for him.

The disciples knew what Jesus meant by this story. While He was away, they must use all that He had given them. They must use their talents and treasures well and wisely. Not one disciple wanted to meet Jesus later with empty hands.

WHAT DO YOU THINK?

1. Which servants could the master trust with his treasure? Which one couldn't he trust?

2. How did the master feel about each of his servants? What did he do for the servants whom he could trust? What about the servant he could not trust?

3. What lesson did the disciples learn from this story? What lesson did you learn from it?

The Love Gift

Maxi Muffin had never heard of a love gift before. Not until his Sunday School teacher said something about a love gift that morning in class.

"Who can tell me the name of the church where we wrote to our pen pals last month?" the teacher asked.

Maxi's hand went up fast. "Cedarville!" he shouted.

"Good, Maxi," said the teacher. "Now who can tell me what happened in Cedarville this week?"

Nobody could. Not even Maxi.

"Well, then," said the teacher, "how many of you heard about the tornadoes this week?"

A few hands went up. Maxi held his up a little, but not very far. He thought he had heard about them, but he wasn't sure.

"Our pastor talked to the pastor in Cedarville yesterday," said the teacher. "Five of the families of our pen pals lost their homes and everything in them. So the mothers and fathers are going to bring

116

some love gifts for these families. Would you like to send some love gifts to your pen pals?"

Some of Maxi's friends looked so puzzled that the teacher thought she should explain about the love gifts. "These should be gifts you *want* to give," said the teacher. "You want to give them because you love someone, not because you want to get rid of something."

"How good should a love gift be?" someone asked.

"That depends on how much love you want to share," the teacher answered. "Love gifts share our love with Jesus as well as His friends."

After class Maxi and his friends all talked about the love gifts that they decided they would give. They weren't sure *what* they should give.

Maxi thought about his love gift all week. On Monday he decided to give his transistor radio because that was his favorite of all his things. But on Tuesday, he began to think about the fun he had with his transistor and decided to give his pocket compass, which was his next-to-favorite thing.

Each day, Maxi thought about his love gift and how much he would miss it. Each day he decided to give something which was a little farther down on his favorite list.

By Sunday morning, Maxi had decided to give a little racing car. He was planning to throw it away soon because it didn't race anymore and one of the wheels was gone.

"Maybe the kid who gets this can ask his dad to fix it," thought Maxi. But he wasn't very happy thinking that way.

Maxi got a lunch bag from the kitchen and put his love gift in it. He put his transistor radio in another lunch bag so he would be ready to visit Pookie after Sunday dinner.

"Hurry and get dressed," said Mommi. "We have to leave by nine so we're not late!"

Maxi hurried to the bathroom and scrubbed his face and combed his hair. Then he quickly put on his clothes and ran to say good-bye to Ruff.

"Don't forget your gift," said Mommi. "But you'd better run. We're almost late!"

Maxi ran into his room, grabbed the lunch bag and hurried out. It always seemed like a race to get to Sunday School!

Maxi had just plopped into his chair when the teacher started the class. "Well, what did we bring for our love gifts?" the teacher asked.

Maxi began to feel a little sorry now about his broken racing car. He clutched his bag tighter and wished that he had brought something a little better.

Then when Maxi saw what some of the others brought, he did feel sorry that he had been so stingy. "You children are certainly showing a lot of love with these gifts," said the teacher. "I know that you all would like to keep the nice things you brought."

Maxi clutched his brown lunch bag tighter. If only he could run home now. He would even like to give his compass, or perhaps even his transistor! He knew that his broken racing car didn't show much love to his pen pal or to Jesus.

"I . . . I'm afraid I didn't show much love with my gift," Maxi said to the teacher. "I'd rather give something better."

Maxi almost shoved the bag into the teacher's hands. He closed his eyes as the teacher reached into the bag to take out his gift.

"Why, Maxi!" said the teacher. "How thoughtful of you! I know this must be your favorite. You are certainly showing a lot of love to give it up."

Maxi could hardly believe his ears. He opened his eyes slowly. There stood the teacher, holding his transistor. Maxi was sure now that if he had two transistors, he would give them both, for that's how much love he wanted to share.

"Thank You, Lord, for helping me grab the wrong bag," Maxi whispered to himself.

LET'S TALK ABOUT THIS

1. Why is it important to give our best to the Lord and His friends?

2. What did Maxi learn about giving his best?

3. What can we give the Lord that is more important than "things"? How can you give Him your time? Your talents? Talk about your talents and how you can use them for the Lord. Your talents may be your singing, playing an instrument, or some other special ability. How can you please God with these?

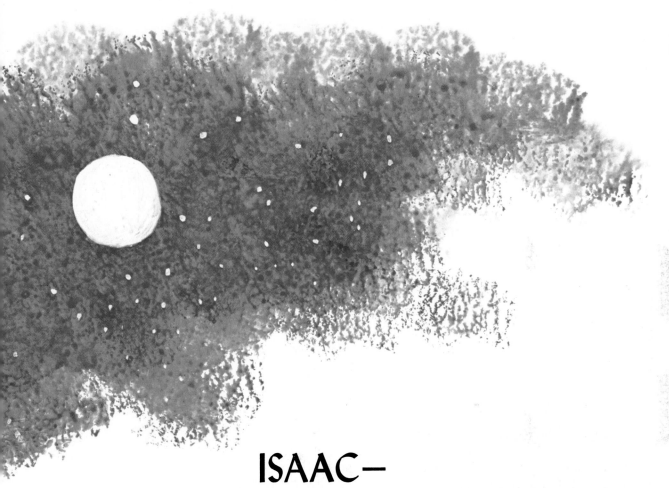

ISAAC–
A PROMISE BENEATH THE STARS

Like the Stars in the Sky

GENESIS 15:1-6; 17:5, 15, 17, 19; 21:1-7

One night, Abram sat beneath the stars, thinking about the one thing he wanted more than anything else in the world.

"If only. . . ." Abram kept thinking, over and over again. But each time he shook his head and sighed. "No, God may never give Sarai and me a son. But if only He would. . . ."

Abram tried to think of something else. He tried to count the stars in the sky. But there were too many.

Suddenly Abram heard a voice speaking. "It is the voice of God!" Abram whispered. He was afraid.

"You must not be afraid," God said to Abram. "I have a wonderful gift for you."

"What good is it to have more gifts when I don't even have a son to inherit what I have now?" Abram asked.

"But that is My gift to you," God told Abram. "You will have a son."

God showed Abram the stars in the night sky above. "Count them!" God said. But Abram knew that he couldn't. He had tried that many times before.

"That's how many children and children's children you will have," God said.

Abram was so happy to hear God's promise. He could hardly wait until his new son would be born.

But Abram did wait. The years passed by and the promised son did not come. At last Abram was an old man.

One day God talked to Abram again. "I have some new names for you and Sarai," He said. "From now on, you will be called Abraham and Sarah."

Then God reminded Abraham of His promise. "You will soon have the new baby I promised you," He said.

"When I'm a hundred years old?" Abraham asked. "And when Sarah is ninety? How can we have a baby when we are so old?"

"But you will," God answered. "By this time next year! And you will call him Isaac, which means 'laughter.'"

Of course it all happened the way God said it would. One day Abraham and Sarah had their new baby.

"We will call him Isaac," said Abraham, "just as God told us to."

"Isaac!" said Sarah. "Laughter! God has helped me laugh today, and my friends to laugh with me. To think that Abraham and I have a new baby boy when we are so old!"

Nobody knows for sure how long Abraham and Sarah laughed as they took their new baby Isaac into their arms. But everyone knows that they were very happy for the wonderful gift that God had given.

WHAT DO YOU THINK?

1. What did Abram want more than anything else in the world?

2. How was Abram's name changed? What wonderful gift did God promise to him then?

3. How did God help Sarah laugh when she was old? What did that have to do with her baby's name?

Pookie's Promises

Pookie's friends were getting a little upset with him. That's because Pookie wasn't keeping his promises.

"But I promise you I'll bring your mitt back this afternoon," Pookie said one day to Maxi. Maxi stayed at home all afternoon waiting for Pookie, but he never came.

"Dumb Pookie," said Maxi. "Just wait! I won't lend my catcher's mitt to him again."

"I'll stop after school and see your rabbits," Pookie said to another friend. "It's a promise!"

But he didn't. "Pookie's promises aren't much good anymore," said the other friend.

"He promised that he would help me carry my goldfish home," said Maria. "But he didn't."

"And he promised to give me some of his Tango Mints," said Mini. "But he ate them all himself."

"Pookie's promises aren't good at all!" said his friends.

Not long after that, Pookie called Maxi on the phone. "Hey, Maxi," he said. "Let's get a baseball game together. I'll call some guys and you call some, and I'll meet you at the park in an hour."

"You will?" asked Maxi.

"It's a promise," said Pookie.

"Forget it," said Maxi. "Your promises aren't good anymore. I'll do something else this afternoon."

Pookie felt sad when he put the phone down. Maxi was right. His promises weren't much good anymore.

Then Pookie called the other friend, and said the same thing to him. But the other friend also asked, "You will?"

"It's a promise," said Pookie.

"Forget it," said the other friend. "Your promises are no good."

Pookie felt very sad now. He knew that he had not been keeping his promises. But what could he do about it this afternoon? Even if he promised that he would keep his promises, his friends wouldn't believe him.

While Pookie stayed home thinking about the promises that he didn't keep, his friends were talking at Maxi's house about Pookie and his promises. "I have an idea," said Maxi. "Will you help me with it?"

The friends were glad to help. So they all went to the phone to call Pookie.

"Pookie," said Maria when she called. "Would you like to see the new pet mouse I just got?"

"Sure," said Pookie. "I'll be over in a few minutes. Will you be home then?" ·

"I promise," said Maria.

Pookie gulped when he heard Maria say that. He didn't feel too good about the word promise.

Just as soon as he hung up the phone, it rang again. This time it was the other friend.

"Hey, Pookie," said the other friend. "Come over and we can get Maxi and play some ball after all."

"OK," said Pookie. "I'll be over as soon as I can. You'll be there, won't you?"

"Sure," said the friend. "I promise."

Pookie gulped harder this time. Why were his friends using that word so often? As soon as he asked his mother about going, he ran down the street for Maria's house.

"Oh, I'm sorry," said her mother. "Maria isn't here. I think she's with Maxi and Mini."

"But she promised!" Pookie grumbled as he walked down the street to his other friend's house. "Why can't people keep their promises?" Then Pookie thought about his own promises and felt sad.

"I'm sorry," said the other friend's mother. "He isn't here now. I think he's with Maxi and Mini."

126

"Then I'll go over there!" Pookie thought. "Why didn't he keep his promise to me?" But as soon as he said that, Pookie thought about his own promises again.

"No, they're not here," said Mommi Muffin when Pookie rang the bell at the Muffin house. "I thought they went to your house to play."

"I just came from there," said Pookie. "They probably went to the park to play without me. They won't play with me anymore because . . . because . . ."

Pookie just couldn't say "because I don't keep my promises." So he ran toward his house, feeling sad. As soon as he went through the gate into his back yard, he heard someone shouting.

"SURPRISE! SURPRISE!" There was Maxi, and Mini, and Maria, and the other friend.

"We're having a promise party," they said. "Want to join us? Whoever comes to the promise party has to keep his promises from now on!"

Pookie was so happy to see his friends. "OK," he said. "I'll keep my promises from now on. Honest I will. I PROMISE!"

Everyone laughed and laughed. Even Pookie. But he really did keep his promises from then on.

LET'S TALK ABOUT THIS

1. In the Bible story, what did God promise Abraham? How did God keep His promises?

2. How did Pookie's friends feel when he didn't keep his promises to them? How did Pookie feel when they didn't keep their promises to him?

3. What should you do when you make promises to your friends? What should you do when you make promises to God?

4. What are some things God has promised to you and your friends? What makes you think He will keep His promises to you? Look up the following and talk about them: Matthew 6:30, Genesis 8:22, Isaiah 1:19, and the last sentence of Hebrews 13:5.

127

The Girl
With the Water Jug

GENESIS 24:1-27

"Look at Isaac!" Abraham thought. "He's a young man now. Soon he will be looking for a bride."

Then Abraham began to look worried. He thought of the girls who lived nearby. There were the Philistine girls. Isaac couldn't marry one of them. They didn't even believe in God.

Then there were the servant girls. But Isaac couldn't marry one of them either. Some day he would be chief of the tribe. In those times, chiefs did not marry servant girls.

"But who else is there?" Abraham wondered.

Then Abraham had an idea. He called his faithful servant, Eliezer, to him.

"Go to Haran," he told Eliezer. "Find a bride for Isaac among my family there."

Eliezer was worried. "What if the girl won't come back with me?" he asked. "What if she won't go so far from home? Should I take Isaac there with me?"

"No!" said Abraham. "You must never take Isaac to Haran. God has promised this land to me and to Isaac. He must stay here."

Eliezer went to work right away. He began giving orders to the other servants.

"Get food for the trip!"

"Find gifts for the bride and her family!"

"Bring ten camels to carry these things."

"Hurry!"

The servants ran here and there, doing what Eliezer told them to do. At last the work was done and Eliezer was ready to leave.

For many days Eliezer rode toward Haran. When he came there at last, he began to think about the best way to find Isaac's bride.

"But who is she?" he wondered. "How will I know her?"

Eliezer found a well outside Haran and waited there until evening. That's when the village girls would come to get water.

Then Eliezer talked to God. "Lord, show me the girl You want Isaac to marry. When the right one comes along, let her water my camels for me."

It would not be easy to find a girl who would water ten thirsty camels. Only a very special girl would offer to do that.

When Eliezer had finished praying, he saw some of the young women of Haran coming to the well. One of them was very beautiful. Eliezer hoped that she would be the one.

"But God must choose Isaac's bride, not me!" Eliezer remembered.

The beautiful young woman came to the well with her water jug. Eliezer ran over to talk to her.

"May I have a drink of water?" he asked.

"Of course," said Rebekah, the beautiful young woman. "I will get water for your camels, too."

"Is this Isaac's bride?" Eliezer wondered. He watched Rebekah as she let her water jug into the well, then poured the water in a trough for the camels to drink. Again and again she did this, so many times that Eliezer stopped counting.

At last the camels had enough. Eliezer was almost sure now that this was the girl that God had chosen. He was so happy that he gave Rebekah a gold earring and two golden bracelets.

"Who is your father?" Eliezer asked.

"Bethuel!" Rebekah answered.

"Bethuel?" Eliezer whispered. "So this is Abraham's family! God has led me to the girl He has chosen for Isaac."

Eliezer bowed his head and talked to God. "Thank You, Lord, for leading me to Abraham's family. But most of all, thank You for showing me the right girl to be Isaac's bride."

WHAT DO YOU THINK?

1. Why did Abraham want Isaac to marry a girl who lived so far away from home? Why couldn't he marry one of the neighbor girls?

2. How did Eliezer find the right girl for Isaac to marry? How did he know that this was the right girl?

3. What did Eliezer do when he found Rebekah?

The Mouse and the Tree House

It wasn't often that Mini could play with a mouse. But someone had given Maria a pet mouse, so Maria wanted to share it with her friend.

"I'm so glad you brought your pet mouse over to my house today," said Mini. "We can play with him in our back yard. Want to play with us, Maxi?"

"Not me," said Maxi, as he climbed into his tree house in the big oak tree. "Who wants to play with a dumb old mouse when he can spot planes going over?"

For a while Maria and Mini kept the mouse in the shoe box that Maria brought him in. But they soon grew tired of doing that and let him out in the grass.

"This is fun," said Maria. "He is playing hide-and-seek with us. Look! He's trying to hide now."

"Then we must look for him," said Mini.

Maria and Mini played hide-and-seek with the pet mouse for a while. "Now, let's close our eyes so he can have a better chance to hide," said Maria. "We will count to five."

132

"One . . . two . . . three . . . four . . . FIVE! Ready or not, here we come!" they said.

But when they looked around, they couldn't see the little mouse at all. He was gone.

Maria and Mini looked here. They looked there. They looked everywhere. But the mouse had won the game of hide-and-seek.

"But I want my pet mouse," said Maria. "We must find him."

"Then why don't you ask me," said Maxi from his tree house.

Mini looked a little angry. "Maxi Muffin, did you take Maria's pet mouse when we weren't looking?"

"No, but I can see him from here," said Maxi. "If you'll be nice, I'll tell you where to find him."

Mini looked all around the yard. She couldn't see the mouse. But Maxi could.

"Go over by the rose bushes," said Maxi.

Maria and Mini ran over to the rose bushes.

"Now turn around and start walking slowly. That's it. Now stop. Look just to your right in that clump of grass."

Just then the little mouse scampered out of the clump of grass. "Ah, we found you," said Mini.

"Yes WE did," chimed Maxi.

MAXI'S CASTLE KNOCK before ENTERING

That night, Mini plopped next to Poppi Muffin and told him all about the mouse and the tree house. "Is that why God sees so many things, 'cause He's up so high?" Mini asked.

"No," said Poppi. "God sees everywhere because He *is* everywhere. You live in your Mini body and look out of two little windows called eyes. But God doesn't need a body, so He can be in many, many places at one time. And He doesn't need eyes like ours to see."

Mini frowned a little and wiggled a lot.

"It's hard to understand, isn't it?" said Poppi.

Mini nodded her head.

"It's hard for any of us to understand, Mini," Poppi went on. "But we know these things are true because God tells us about them in His Word. God can see a lot better and a lot more than Maxi could see from his tree house. So we should ask Him to show us what to do and where to go each day."

"Then I suppose that's what I should do right now," said Mini. So she did.

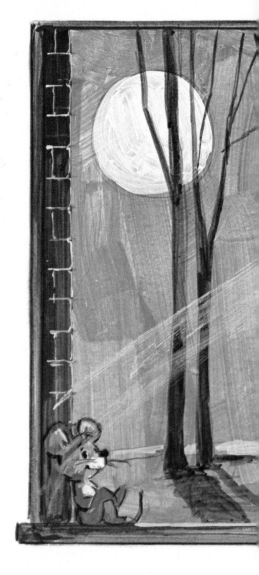

LET'S TALK ABOUT THIS

1. Why do we ask God to show us what to do? Why do you think Eliezer asked God to show him the right person for Isaac? If we don't know what is ahead, why should we ask God for help?

2. How much do you know about the things that will happen tomorrow? Next week? Who does? If God knows all these things, how can He help you? Will you ask Him now?

The Man
Who Would Not Fight

GENESIS 26:13-33

"You must move away," King Abimelech told Isaac. "We do not want you here with us."

Isaac was very sad to hear the king say this. He wanted to be friends with the Philistines. But the Philistines did not like a neighbor who had more sheep and cattle than they had.

"Why can't they see that God gave me all these things?" Isaac thought.

Isaac's servants were angry. "We should fight these Philistines," they said. "We should make them move away instead of us."

"No," said Isaac. "We will not fight them. We can never be their friends if we do. We will move to a new place."

So Isaac and his servants moved their animals and their tents to a new place nearby. It was a place where Isaac's father, Abraham, had once lived.

"There will be water here," Isaac said. "My father dug many wells when I was a boy."

But Isaac was sad when he saw his father's wells. They were filled with dirt.

"The Philistines did this!" Isaac's servants shouted. "Let's fight them!"

"We will not fight the Philistines," said Isaac. "We will dig the dirt from these wells. Then we will dig a new well, too."

It was hard work to dig the dirt from the old wells. It was even harder work to dig a new well. When Isaac's servants finished digging the new well, they saw men coming toward them.

"The Philistines!" they shouted. "What do they want?"

"We want our well," said the Philistines. "This is our land, so it is our well."

Isaac's men became angry. The Philistines became angry, too. Everyone began to argue and shout and say things that shouldn't have been said.

"Stop, stop!" said Isaac. "We will not argue and fight with you. We will move farther away and dig a new well."

Isaac's men grumbled as they moved away to a new place. They grumbled as they dug a new well. But they were happy at last when the well was finished.

Then they saw the Philistines coming again. This time Isaac's men began to fight with the Philistines.

"You must not do that," said Isaac. "We will move even farther from the Philistines. We will dig another new well."

Isaac's men grumbled and complained more than they had before as they moved to the new place. They were angry as they dug a new well.

As soon as they were finished, Isaac's men stood around the new well, waiting for the Philistines. But the Philistines never came.

"Perhaps Isaac was right," said the servants. "Now we can spend our time doing the right things instead of fighting."

That night God talked with Isaac. "Do not be afraid of Me," God said. "I will do many good things for you."

Isaac knew then that he had done what God wanted him to do. So he built an altar where he and his people could worship God.

Not long after that, King Abimilech came to see Isaac. The commander of the Philistine army came with him, along with a man named Ahuzzath.

Isaac's men were afraid now. "See," they said. "The Philistines will try to make us move again."

"Why have you come to see us?" Isaac asked. "Do you want to cause more trouble?"

"No," said King Abimelech. "We want to be your friends. We see now that God is with you."

Isaac was happy that he had not fought with the Philistines. So were his servants.

"It is better to make friends than to fight enemies," said Isaac's servants. "Now God has given us new water, new land, and new friends."

So Isaac and his people thanked God for all these new gifts.

WHAT DO YOU THINK?

1. Why were the Philistines jealous of Isaac at first? What did Isaac have that they did not have (Genesis 26:12-14)? Who gave him all these things?

2. If Isaac had fought the Philistines, how would this story have changed? Pretend that he did fight them, then tell this story to your mother or father. Which story has a happier ending, the pretend one or the real one?

Mini Muffin
Says Nothing

"Dumb sister!" Maxi grumbled. "Why didn't you tell me that was a rock?"

Mini Muffin wanted to tell Maxi that he was the dumb one. Couldn't he tell a toadstool from a rock? And did he have to kick it so hard that he almost hurt Ruff and Tuff?

But Mini Muffin said nothing.

Everything had seemed like so much fun when Mini and Maxi had packed the lunch basket for their picnic in the woods. Now Maxi was like a grouchy old bear. And it was all his own fault. Mini wanted to tell Maxi a thing or two.

But Mini Muffin said nothing.

"Why don't you carry this dumb basket?" Maxi growled. "You're not carrying a thing except that old blanket."

Maxi set the basket by a big rock and walked on ahead. Mini picked it up and walked fast to catch up with him. Ruff and Tuff had to run to keep up.

Mini wanted to say some things that little sisters shouldn't ever say to their big brothers.

But Mini Muffin said nothing.

Maxi was still talking about his dumb sister when they passed under a big limb on an old tree. Maxi picked up a rock and pointed to a gray lump of something hanging from the limb.

"Watch me!" said Maxi. "One pitch and a HOME RUN!"

Maxi shouted "HOME RUN" as he threw the rock. The big gray lump fell to the ground.

Suddenly the air was filled with loud, angry buzzing. The buzzing grew louder and angrier.

"Hornets!" they both shouted, running as fast as they could. Ruff and Tuff ran even faster.

"Home run!" thought Mini.

But Mini Muffin said nothing.

At last Mini and Maxi came to a beautiful place under the trees. Squirrels jumped in the branches. Birds sang in the tops of the trees. And rabbits played tag by a big bed of flowers.

"This looks like a good place," said Maxi. "Let's eat. I'm starved."

Mini spread out the blanket and put some sandwiches and potato chips out for them to eat. But while they were watching the rabbits, a hungry squirrel stole some of the potato chips.

"Dumb sister," said Maxi. "Why did you put them there? And why don't you pray for the food?"

Mini Muffin said nothing—to Maxi. But she began to talk to God.

"Dear God," she said, "help Maxi to know that I love him and don't want to quarrel with him. And bless our potato chips and sandwiches. Amen."

Mini started to munch on a potato chip. But Maxi did nothing.

He didn't eat a sandwich. He didn't eat a potato chip. He just looked at Mini.

"I'm sorry," said Maxi. "I've been sorta dumb. Why don't you tell me off?"

Of course, Mini Muffin said nothing. But she did give Maxi a big smile. Then she and Maxi had the best picnic ever with Ruff and Tuff.

LET'S TALK ABOUT THIS

1. Why did Mini Muffin say nothing? Are there times when you should say nothing, too?

2. Has someone said some unkind things to you lately? What did you do? What will you do the next time someone says unkind things to you?

3. If Mini Muffin had argued and shouted at Maxi, how would this story have been different? How can things be different in your home if you learn to say nothing instead of arguing?

Mini's Word List

Sixteen words that all Minis and Maxis want to know.

APOSTLE—One of the twelve special men Jesus chose to work closely with Him. When Judas was dead, another man, Matthias, took his place. Paul also was an apostle because Jesus chose him to do a special work, too.

BRICKS—Like our bricks, the Egyptian bricks were used to make buildings. But they were made of mud and were much larger.

BULRUSHES—Plants that grew near the water, such as a river. They were a kind of reed.

CHARIOT—A cart with two wheels, pulled by horses. It was used for fighting or to take important people somewhere.

FAMINE—A time when there was little or no food. Usually a famine came when there was no rain and crops did not grow.

FORGIVE—To not hold something against a person anymore, even to forget it.

GLEAN—Poor people could follow Bible-time reapers and gather the stalks of grain they missed.

HEBREW—One of the descendants of Jacob and his twelve sons. Also called the Children of Israel, for Israel was another name for Jacob.

INHERIT—What a child gets from his parents, usually when the parents die.

LEPROSY—A disease that brought white spots to the skin. Sometimes the toes or fingers shriveled. Leprosy could be "caught" from another person.

MIDIAN—A land east of Egypt and south of Israel.

PHARISEE—One of the religious leaders in Jesus' time. They did not like Jesus because He said He was God's Son.

SLAVE—Someone who was forced to work for another person, usually without pay.

TASKMASTER—A man who made slaves do their work.

THRESHING FLOOR—A flat place on the ground where people beat grain from the stalks. There they also separated the grain from the chaff.

VINEYARD—A place where grapes were grown on vines.